OSLG

A SUMMER IN TUSCANY

Emma is an art restorer, sent to the de Luca estate by her boss. Delighted by the charms of Tuscany and involved in her work, the last thing on her mind is romance. But Leandro — the tall, dark and handsome owner of the estate — increasingly finds his way into her thoughts. Swearing not to mix business with pleasure, Emma struggles in vain to deny her growing feelings. However, Leandro's childhood friend Mariella wants him too — and she's prepared to go to any lengths to get him . . .

Books by Wendy Kremer
in the Linford Romance Library:

REAP THE WHIRLWIND
AT THE END OF THE RAINBOW
WHERE BLUEBELLS GROW WILD
WHEN WORDS GET IN THE WAY
COTTAGE IN THE COUNTRY
WAITING FOR A STAR TO FALL
SWINGS AND ROUNDABOUTS
KNAVE OF DIAMONDS
SPADES AND HEARTS
TAKING STEPS
I'LL BE WAITING
HEARTS AND CRAFTS
THE HEART SHALL CHOOSE
THE HOUSE OF RODRIGUEZ
WILD FRANGIPANI
TRUE COLOURS

WENDY KREMER

A SUMMER
IN TUSCANY

Complete and Unabridged

LINFORD
Leicester

First published in Great Britain in 2014

First Linford Edition
published 2015

A catalogue record for this book is available
from the British Library.

ISBN 978–1–4448–2551–0

Published by
F. A. Thorpe (Publishing)
Anstey, Leicestershire

Set by Words & Graphics Ltd.
Anstey, Leicestershire
Printed and bound in Great Britain by
T. J. International Ltd., Padstow, Cornwall

This book is printed on acid-free paper

1

As Emma got out of the jeep, a horseman on a powerful black stallion galloped into the courtyard. As he stopped and brought the temperamental horse under control, she couldn't help noting he was very good-looking with angular features and neatly cut dark hair. Emma had already seen a rider racing along the crest of one of the fields as she drove up the dusty road to the house. It must have been him.

Another man crossed the cobbled yard and came towards her. He said something to her in Italian, noticed her puzzled expression, and then glanced at the number plate. Smiling, he asked politely in English, 'Can I help you? Have you lost your way?'

She shook her head and smiled. 'No I don't think so! I'm expected. My name is Emma Lomax. I'm from Maurice Holsworth.'

The horseman threw a leg over the saddle and jumped down. She remained outwardly undaunted, although the proximity of the animal, its size and restless prancing, made her nervous. His dark brown eyes gazed at her candidly and their straightforwardness disconcerted her a little. He glanced at her jeep and then asked, 'You've come from Maurice Holsworth? Where's Mr. Holsworth?'

Her throat was dry and she tried to sound assertive. 'Good afternoon.' She held out her hand. He took it in his for a brief moment. 'I'm Emma Lomax. Leandro de Luca has commissioned us to restore some paintings. He's expecting Maurice, but unfortunately he's delayed.'

He sounded impatient. 'What does that mean? I'm Leandro de Luca.'

His English was excellent with hardly a trace of an accent and she saw he was used to making decisions and giving orders. For some illogical reason, she'd envisaged Leandro de Luca as a middle-aged courteous aristocrat with salt-and-pepper hair. She hastened to explain. 'I'm Maurice's assistant. Maurice broke his leg in two places the day before yesterday. He didn't want to let you down; and as he is unable to travel at present, and won't be fit enough for several weeks, he sent me to replace him.'

A shadow of annoyance crossed his face and he said impatiently, 'I arranged for Mr. Holsworth to handle the paintings. I'm sorry about his mishap but we never considered, or talked about, him sending a substitute if it was necessary. Are you a qualified art restorer?'

She steeled herself and met his glance. Was he was just another arrogant employer who assumed that because she was female she was less capable? She appeared outwardly unperturbed when she replied, 'Yes, I'm fully qualified and very experienced! I've worked for Maurice ever since I qualified, five years ago.'

He eyed her and slapped his gloved hand with his riding whip. The muscles rippled under his shirt. 'I only have your word for that. Would you allow an unknown stranger to work on family paintings without some kind of an assurance? I checked up on Maurice and spoke to some of his previous clients before I decided to employ him. I don't know anything about you.'

Emma hadn't driven all this way for nothing. She had to win him over. 'Everyone thinks Maurice deals with everything himself, but that's not always the case. Maurice often has too many commissions to deal with single-handed. I belong to a team of restorers who share the work with him. I may have even worked on one of those jobs you checked, without the owner knowing it. You can be certain that he wouldn't have sent me if he thought I didn't have enough skill or ability. He has to consider his reputation. He didn't want to disappoint you. As soon as he's able to travel, he plans to replace me. You have my word that I'll handle your pictures with great care and restore them without damaging them. That's what I'm trained to do.'

There was a moment of silence, and he considered her carefully. He ran his hand through his thick hair and it sprang back into place. His expression was un-wavering. 'I presume he's at home? Give me his private number, please.'

She grabbed her satchel to search for Maurice's home number and her blond hair flopped forward and hid her annoyed expression. She copied it onto a piece of paper, and with heightened colour she handed it to him.

He took it and then handed the horse's reins to the other man before he walked towards the house without another word.

What an arrogant, haughty, objec-tionable man. She'd remained polite for Maurice's sake but wouldn't care one bit if he came back and told her to clear off again. Emma took a deep breath and looked at her surroundings to hide her irritation.

The villa was large and obviously old. It had rust-coloured walls that glowed in the sunshine. The overhanging tiled roof provided a fringe of shade from the glaring sun. Opposite the forecourt was a hedged-in garden with a wrought-iron entrance gate.

The younger man smiled at her playfully and studied her face. He tied the reins to a ring in the wall and said, 'Don't take any notice. Leandro isn't unfriendly. He just takes anything, and everything, to do with the estate much too seriously. I think a very attractive female with green eyes and blond hair is infinitely more acceptable than a middle-aged male restorer. I don't understand why he's bothering about the pictures in the first place. Most of them are dismal and depressing.'

She buried her annoyance. 'Lots of old paintings are dreary to modern-day eyes, especially ones with mystical or religious motives. The people who commissioned them centuries ago wanted to impress others with their wealth, or they hoped to buy off their sins in the eyes of God. Perhaps Mr. de Luca is worried that his ancestors will end up in everlasting purgatory if I damage one of them.' She smiled at him. 'You know my name. You are?'

'Marco de Luca.' He bowed with artificial aplomb and barely touched the back of her hand with his lips. It was a continental gesture, totally foreign to British men. 'Leandro is my brother.'

Emma noted the flirtatious manner and his twinkling eyes. He was completely in character with her idea of Italian manhood.

Marco cast an approving glance at her shapely figure in her blue jeans and loose indigo T-shirt and was about to say something else when a middle-aged woman emerging from the shadows of the house interrupted them.

Marco turned to her. 'Mama, this is Emma. She has come to restore the paintings . . . if Leandro lets her.'

The woman smiled at him indulgently. Her olive skin was smooth and her hair was dark and streaked with grey. Her soft white blouse flowed softly over her breasts, and her black figure-skimming trousers were well-cut and stylish.

She held out her hand to Emma. 'I'm Zarah de Luca. Leandro informed me in passing that you were here. It is very ill-mannered of him to leave you standing in the sun. Welcome to the Villa Bella Rosa. Come inside and have something to drink.'

'Thank you. I'd like that.' She followed her, and Marco fell into step behind them.

Over her shoulder, his mother uttered, 'Marco, you promised to help Paola load her van so that she can leave for the market at the break of dawn tomorrow. I think I can entertain our English visitor without your help.'

He grinned at Emma and shrugged his shoulders before he said 'Ciao!' and turned away.

Emma followed his mother through some French windows into a cool dining room with a large oval dining table and heavy side furniture. They crossed the neighbouring flagstoned hallway into another larger room overlooking an inner courtyard with cool greenery.

Zarah de Luca gestured her towards a comfortable settee. Emma's knowledgeable glance noted the paintings, costly antique lamps, knick-knacks, and valuable cabinets. An ancient wood-burning fireplace in the stonework wall dominated the whole room.

Emma remarked, 'What a superb fireplace, and what a magnificent house.'

Signora de Luca smiled. 'I must admit I love that fireplace too. In past centuries it was probably the main source of heat on colder days, apart from the ovens in the kitchen. The house is typical for this region. It hasn't changed much since it was built. The de Luca family owned large tracts of land around here centuries ago. They supported the Medici. Leandro is doing his best to hang on to what's left.'

An older woman came in with a tray and arranged some tea things on the table.

'I hope tea is all right? You can have something else, if you prefer.'

'Tea is lovely, thank you.'

With a glance at Emma, the serving woman withdrew.

Emma accepted a dainty cup with a gold rim and said, 'Tuscany is beautiful. I passed numerous fantastic spots on the way here.'

'People who live in Tuscany tend to take it for granted. It's our workplace and our home, but we're still extremely proud of it. It is beautiful.' She gestured to the tea things on the tray. 'Help yourself to milk sugar, or lemon. Did you have a good journey?'

'Yes, thank you. I've never driven so far on my own before, but the GPS system is a godsend. If I took a wrong turn, it soon guided me back again.'

'I don't drive long distances any-more, so I don't need one.'

Emma took a sip of tea. 'This is very good. I'm very surprised how well you and your sons speak English.'

She smiled at Emma briefly. 'I went to a strict convent school. My sons went to an international school and stayed in England for a while, with some relatives. English is the world's main language these days, isn't it? I hope you're looking forward to working here.'

Emma didn't want to involve her in a potential wrangle between her son and herself. 'Who wouldn't? It's the cradle of the European Renaissance.'

'Restoring art is an unusual profession for a woman, isn't it?'

'Not really. Not these days.' She leaned forward and with a touch of camaraderie in her voice, she said, 'I think women are very suited to it, because we have more patience.'

The older woman laughed softly. 'Well, I agree with you there. You seem to like your work.'

'I do. I love it.'

'I gather something has prevented Maurice Holsworth from coming?' Emma explained what had happened. 'What bad luck! Still, I'm sure he wouldn't have sent you unless you were skilled.'

Emma laughed softly. 'I tried to convince your son of that, but I don't think he believed me. He's gone to check with Maurice.'

Zarah's silver bracelet jingled. 'Oh, that's typical. My husband was still young when he died — a fatal car accident. Leandro had to step into his shoes when he should still have been enjoying himself. He runs the estate like a well-oiled machine, and his head is full of plans for tomorrow, next year, and the one after that too. He's too preoccupied with it, and too involved in every detail. In contrast, nothing worries Marco. Sometimes I wonder how I managed to produce such different characters.'

There was sound of heavy footsteps in the hall signalling Leandro's return.

Tension had coloured their first encounter, but that didn't mean Emma wasn't aware that he was an extremely attractive man with an interesting personality. His washed-out jeans hugged his slim hips and his tailored check shirt, with sleeves rolled up to his elbows, stretched tightly across his broad shoulders.

'I've spoken to Maurice. He recommends you and assures me that you're one of the very best, so I'm willing to give you a try.'

The way he said it sounded almost derisive, but Emma preferred frank and honest people, even if they jumped unthinkingly on her toes. Now that she'd adjusted to the situation, she was too professional not to understand why this man had first confirmed things with Maurice. Restoration work on valuable paintings was always a question of trust. She looked at him and got up. 'I promise I'll do a good job.'

The dark eyes narrowed, and he studied her like a hawk for a moment. His stance and his expression prompted her to reflect and realize that he came from an ancient line of proud, aristocratic men. He held out his hand with its long fingers. 'Let's shake on it, shall we?'

Emma took it and for some reason she was relieved that they'd reached a mutual understanding, and that she'd be staying here after all.

2

Leandro viewed the tea things briefly and then said, 'If you like, I'll show you your workplace and the paintings.'

Emma nodded and, for a moment, his dark chocolate eyes distracted her. She explained her confusion by telling herself how much she loved dark chocolate.

His mother commented, 'Leandro, she's only just arrived. Give her a chance to finish her tea.'

He smiled at her, and the expression changed his looks completely. Something in Emma stirred and she told herself not to be so adolescent. Italy and Tuscany were having an idiotic effect on her. This was a job like any other.

His voice sounded friendlier and there was a touch of amusement in his eyes when he said, 'I do not have my whip with me anymore, and I had no intention of parting Miss Lomax from her teacup.'

Emma drank the remains in her cup hastily. She turned to him. 'It's fine with me. I'm here to work.' She looked across at his mother. 'Thank you for the tea; it was just what I needed.'

'You're welcome! Don't let Leandro bully you.'

Emma glanced at him and away quickly. 'I won't. I don't let anyone bully me. The sooner I start, the sooner I'll finish, and the sooner I'll get out from under your feet again. Perhaps Maurice will replace me faster than anyone expects.'

Signora de Luca viewed them as Emma followed him out. She was an intelligent, polite young woman, and she had an agreeable manner. It would be good to have another female around the house. The prospect of having her as a working guest for a while was quite a pleasant one after all.

Emma hurried to catch up with Leandro. He paused at the main door and held it open. She sidled past him and kept up with his long strides as they went along the side of the house towards a group of detached outhouses. On the way, he asked her politely about her journey. Emma hid her amusement at his obvious attempt to smooth any lingering ruffled feathers.

They reached what had once probably been a large storage shed or barn. Substantial new doors had replaced old ones. Their wooden panels glistened like golden honey in the afternoon sun. She followed him inside. The room was enormous.

'I hope you don't mind those things being there?' He gestured towards some table-tennis equipment and other playthings along one of the walls. 'The children have fun with them sometimes and I don't have any other suitable place to put them at present.'

Emma's lungs deflated briefly with a feeling of disappointment. He had children? He was married? She told herself it made no real difference, but she wished Maurice had supplied her with more details about the family. She did know that Leandro de Luca hadn't wanted the paintings moved, and that was why they had to come here to restore them. Before she left, Maurice and she hadn't had time for tittle-tattle or for him to give her more information.

Emma looked around. 'No, there's plenty of room. It's dry and clean. I've more space here than I have in London. If I need to keep it dust-free, I can always seal off an area with some sheets.'

'You can open the doors when it gets too hot, and there are some small windows at the back for ventilation. I could have given you a room in the house, but I thought this would be quieter, and the lighting is better too.'

She smiled at him. 'You're right. It's

perfect and it's out of other people's way.'

He stuck one hand in his pocket. 'Would you like to see the paintings?' He hesitated. 'Or perhaps you'd like to unpack and adjust to your new surrounding first?'

'No. I've been sitting in the jeep all day and I'm curious to see what Maurice thought needed attention.'

'Right. Then follow me!'

They returned to the house, crossed the hall, and went up a substantial, solidly carved staircase. At the top he turned left down a long corridor, and Emma followed him. Paintings hung along its length, and statues and sculptures stood in window niches that looked down into the inner courtyard. He let her wander for a while on her own.

There was an assortment of old and modern paintings, and a lot more than she expected. She examined some of them closely. 'Wow! You have some lovely paintings, and there are some very interesting contrasting styles. I bet some are quite valuable.'

He joined her. 'So I'm told. No one has added anything in my lifetime, but earlier generations seem to have bought them continually whenever they had money to spare.'

She nodded. 'Paintings have always been one of the main methods of decorating walls. These days art collectors often only see them as investments, or something to flaunt in front of others. I think that's a great shame.'

Over her shoulder, he contemplated the one she was examining and said in a casual, jesting way, 'Marco claims most of ours are disgustingly depressing and insists that our family has always had misguided tastes.'

Emma laughed and shrugged. 'So I gather! It's all a question of era and taste. Sometimes motifs in the past were dark and gloomy, other times they were flooded with colour and light. I'm guessing that a lot of your paintings are quite valuable, even if Marco isn't impressed. What made you decide they deserved some attention?'

'I read about Maurice holding a talk at a local art gallery. I knew we had to do something about this lot one day, so I went along just to find out what was involved. He offered a free judgement and picked out three that he said needed most help. He said all of them could do with some attention, but he didn't push that point. He just encouraged me to think about starting with these three. I liked his attitude and that he didn't even mind when I said I didn't want them moved.'

'That's one reason Maurice is so successful. People like him because he's very honest.' The corridor was full of shadows because of the overhanging roof. She glanced out of the windows. 'Marco might appreciate the paintings better when the surface dirt is removed. I'm glad you've hung them away from the windows and sources of heat. Stable conditions keep the varnish stable for much longer.'

He nodded. 'Maurice said the same thing. I don't suppose our ancestors realized that, but I think they've always hung in roughly the same place as they do now. Like to see the ones Maurice chose?'

'Gladly!'

He went ahead and pointed. 'This one, the one next to it, and the last one, down the end of the corridor.'

Emma studied them. 'Hm! This is very attractive, even if it's a lot darker than when it was painted.' She looked at the neighbouring one. 'In contrast, this is quite modern — by a well-known early nineteenth-century French artist. I can understand why Maurice put it at the top of his list. I already feel privileged to handle them.' She went to examine the final one. Emma could see that it was in the worst condition of all. 'I don't recognize the artist and it's hard to even guess what's on it. Who's it by?'

He came to look over her shoulder. 'It's supposed to be by Dossi, and that would make it very valuable, but no one has ever been certain. Maurice seemed sure there's something worthwhile under all that grime.'

She wracked her brain for information. 'The Venetian painter, Dossi? He's not very well known, but he was famous in his day for his unusual use of light. Most of his known paintings are badly damaged, but they're still very valuable.'

Leandro relaxed and felt more comfortable with her. 'That's right.' He shrugged. 'Apparently we'd need all kinds of expensive tests and assessments by experts to establish that it is a real Dossi. My father thought about doing so, but was always afraid more damage would be done by taking it away, than just never knowing the truth.' The corner of his mouth turned up. 'I often wondered if he just didn't want to hear that it wasn't worth the canvas it was painted on. It is old, though; anyone can see that.'

They stood side-by-side in front of

the picture. 'And you don't mind me handling it anymore?'

He turned and smiled. 'Taking it across to the workshop means it stays here, and I have the feeling you know your job. I must apologize for my ill-mannered reception. No doubt my mother will bend my ear next time I see her. I often forget that my direct approach sometimes dismays people. Welcome to the Villa Bella Rosa, Emma! I hope I may call you Emma?'

Emma's mood improved. The hush of centuries settled around them. Her heart skipped a beat. 'Yes, please do.' Her early-warning system reminded her that he was a married man with children. He was off-limits. She wasn't here for a romantic adventure with anyone. She was almost glad when he turned away and headed back down the corridor.

Over his shoulder he exclaimed, 'Let's find out where Franca has decided to put you for the duration of your stay, then you can unpack and have a little time to yourself before the evening meal. Did Marco tie my horse up properly?'

She nodded. 'I'm no judge because I know nothing about knots, but I think so.'

The corners of his mouth turned up. 'Good! He gets upset if I leave him standing around too long. The horse, not Marco.'

Downstairs again in the entrance hall, he shouted, 'Franca!'

Someone shuffled down a corridor from the depths of the house; it was the woman who'd served the tea. She looked favourably at Leandro and her eyes twinkled. She was short, with slightly rounded shoulders and a severe bun crowning her head. She had a pleasant face and was wearing a sparkling white apron.

'Will you show Emma to her room, please?'

Franca gave him a barely-visible nod and then preceded Emma up the stairs again. Without a backward glance, he

25

left her and headed for the door. Emma sprinted to catch up with Franca. They turned right at the top of the stairs and went down another corridor. Franca stopped in front of the appropriate door.

'This is your room. I'll open the window to let in some fresh air.' She did so and a smell of geraniums flooded the room. I'll get my husband, Enzo, to fetch your suitcase.'

Emma looked around. 'It's lovely, thank you! Please don't bother your husband. I'll fetch it myself. I'm here to work. I don't expect you, or your husband, to wait on me. I'm sure you already have enough to do.'

Franca gave her a tentative smile and fiddled with her apron. 'We've been with the de Lucas for nearly thirty years. We like it here. They are our family.'

'Where did you learn to speak such good English? I'm surprised how many people in this house do — and I'm very relieved, because my Italian is non-existent.'

26

'We ran a small hotel and had a lot of English guests before we came here. But working for the de Luca family is a lot easier than running a hotel.'

They walked side-by-side back downstairs. Franca explained, 'My husband does whatever is needed. He tends the garden, does repairs around the place, helps Leandro during harvesting, helps me with the cooking most days, and looks after the stables. I think he enjoys it here because the work is so varied and because he can more or less decide what to do independently. It feels a bit like our hotel without the responsibility.'

They parted in the hall. Emma pulled her suitcase out of the back of the jeep and went back upstairs. She had barely opened the lid and put her underwear in one of the drawers when a knock on the door announced Franca's return. In her arms she had a bundle of soft white towels.

'The bathroom is next door. If you need anything else just ask.'

'Thanks! What time is the evening meal, and where?'

'Roughly eight o'clock. I think you came through the dining room on the way in, didn't you? It's at the bottom of the stairs on the left.'

'The whole family will be there? Signora De Luca, Marco, Leandro, his wife and children?'

Franca looked at her with widened eyes and began to chuckle. 'Leandro's wife? Children? The only children I've ever seen here are Rosella's.'

She was too curious not to ask further. 'Rosella?'

'She's Marco and Leandro's sister. She married a diplomat nearly ten years ago and they have two children, Asella and Antonio.'

'Oh, I see.' Emma wondered why she felt relieved. 'He told me the toys in the shed were the children's. I assumed he meant his own children.'

Franca's laughter cackled. 'I'll have to tell Zarah that; she'll enjoy the joke. Leandro, a father? I've been waiting for that to happen for twenty years. I hope he gets round to it soon, so that I see his children before I die.' Shaking her head and still chuckling, she exited and shut the door quietly behind her.

3

It had been an unusual day. In the washroom off the hall, Leandro de Luca scrubbed his hands and then applied some strong ointment to a couple of long scratches he'd picked up hacking away at some overgrown creepers that morning. He'd looked at his watch and decided there was still enough time to go for a ride before he freshened up for the evening meal. Warrior needed the exercise and he needed some time on his own to think.

The afternoon haze was lying like a blanket on the land as he cantered to the top of the nearby hill. At ease on his favourite stallion, he looked around the place where he'd been born and grown up. It was hard work making enough money to maintain the estate. The upkeep of the house and the farm left next to nothing for all the other things he planned. Still, they were making progress. Their Chianti had won prizes in the last couple of years and it was improving constantly. Vincenzo, their winemaker, was producing superior wines, better than others from the Chianti area. Leandro wished he had more spare time to learn the secrets of winemaking from Vincenzo, but he had to handle the olive and sunflower production. They were just as important, and an essential source of income.

If and when Marco decided to join him in running the estate, he'd have more time to relax, but until then he'd manage as best as he could. Marco should have the chance to merely enjoy life that he hadn't had at that age. A smile flitted across his face. Marco was a flirt, with a sunny disposition. He'd lost count of Marco's past girlfriends. Everyone liked him and he cultivated an interesting assortment of friendships wherever he went. Mother would never admit it, but she was putty in his hands.

Recently Marco had surprised him

when he suggested they could convert some disused buildings near the turnoff from the main highway into holiday homes. He'd even persuaded an architect friend of his to work out the rough cost of conversion. It was a sign he was taking interest in the place. A promising one.

The idea wasn't a bad one. A couple of holiday homes could provide a steady form of extra income for years to come. Everyone else was taking advantage of the storm of tourists. And why shouldn't they, as long as it didn't change anything at the villa? The buildings in question were closer to the village than to Villa Bella Rosa, so visitors weren't likely to bother them too much. Most neighbouring families had already turned their former homes into apartment buildings. Some had added swimming pools and made attractive surrounding gardens. They'd deserted their family homes and moved into smaller modern ones in nearby villages or towns.

Perhaps it was just as well that as he was the older one, it had fallen to him to guide the fate of Villa Bella Rosa when his father died. Marco might have turned it into a harbourage for his waifs and strays or given in and let tourism run riot. Eventually Villa Bella Rosa might have ended up as just another luxury hotel, and he didn't intend to let that happen — not ever.

He brought his horse to a standstill and the bridle jingled as Warrior chaffed to be on the move again. Viewing the surrounding landscape for the umpteenth time, he admired how his ancestors had positioned the villa perfectly on the crest of the hill. Embedded in the summit, it was part of a wonderful panorama. His glance flowed across the groves of old olive trees and the ripening sunflowers in the fields. It was a scene he'd grown up with, and never ceased to love. No one sensed how much he loved the Villa Bella Rosa. Well perhaps his mother did, because she'd worked alongside him to protect it as best they could. It was part of him, and looking after it took precedence over everything else in his life.

He continued to gaze across the landscape around the villa. The Land Rover parked outside the house caught his attention. He checked the nervous movements of his favourite horse and thought about the English woman.

His initial reaction hadn't intimidated her, and she knew her own mind. He liked that. She was very attractive too, and seemed to know what she was doing. He wondered how she'd fit into their daily routine. She was only here for a limited time, but a stranger in the family was bound to cause some disruption. Perhaps Maurice really would replace her sooner than anyone expected.

The restoration work on the paintings was something else that would drain their spare revenue, but Maurice had convinced him that if they didn't do something to preserve some of the pictures soon, they might be lost to future generations. He pulled at the harness, gave his horse a slight tap with his boots, and directed it back towards the house with a clicking sound.

4

The evening meal was delicious, and by Emma's usual standards it was lavish. The atmosphere was very relaxed. Marco was out but Leandro and his mother tried to make her feel comfortable. They talked about the region, the neighbouring estates and local history, and asked about her job and her family. They encouraged her to try a little of all the local dishes Franca had cooked for them, and they all tasted wonderful.

Emma wondered if they minded having a stranger at their table. They didn't seem bothered; but she'd be around for a couple of weeks, and it was bound to restrict their private lives and hamper confidential conversation sometimes. But they also knew she didn't understand Italian, so if necessary they could still exchange important personal information that way. When a large stoneware platter with tempting local cheeses and fresh bread arrived, she left. She explained she just couldn't eat any more.

Placing her folded serviette neatly to one side, she said, 'Thank you for the meal. It was delicious. I think I'll have an early night tonight so I'm fresh to start working tomorrow. Is my jeep in anyone's way?'

Leandro lowered his knife and eyed her. 'No, you can leave it where it is. Park it alongside your workplace tomorrow. *Buonanotte*!'

She gave both of them a parting smile. '*Buonanotte*!'

* * *

Upstairs in her room, she was drawn to the open window. Emma's enthusiasm grew as she viewed the spread of the fantastic Tuscan countryside in the colours of the setting sun. Who could fail to be impressed by the gentle rolling hills and the elegant rows of cypress trees? It felt like she was in the midst of an historical pageant. She reminded herself that she had come here to work, but that didn't lessen the feeling that she was somewhere that took her breath away.

She thought back to when Maurice had unexpectedly woken her at the crack of dawn two days ago to tell her she had to replace him because he'd fallen over his cat, broken his leg in two places, and cracked some ribs. At the time, she'd protested, and tried to refuse to go. She was happy in London, spoke no Italian, and she had plenty of work to keep her busy at home.

Pulling a chair closer, she now settled her arms on the window frame and thanked fate for bringing her here. Basically, the work was a commission just like any other — but it wasn't. It was in Tuscany, and that made it very different. Maurice had kept begging for her to take over and she gave in. He was a good boss and a nice person. Emma couldn't let him down. She'd learned almost everything she knew about restoring art from Maurice, and they got on well. She knew he'd been looking forward to doing the job himself. His wife was going to join him at the end of the work and they were planning to stay near Florence for a short holiday. He'd been clearly annoyed that his plans were all shattered and he couldn't do the work himself.

Re-booking the journey, organizing who'd finish her half-finished work, arranging Maurice's work and his appointments kept them all busy. There wasn't much time for Emma to gather much personal information about her future employer before she left. She only knew the family was old and aristocratic and their client, Leandro de Luca, was a marquis, but no one called him by that title. Maurice said he was a nice chap. Emma was beginning to understand why Maurice thought so. The journey had been uneventful, and her journey through the Chianti region memorable, because of the scenery.

Pictures she's seen of it didn't do it justice.

Emma left the window and got ready for bed. She thought briefly about her tasks tomorrow. She had to set up a workplace and take a closer look at the paintings. If she was lucky, she might be able to make a start on one of them. She drifted off into a deep and dreamless sleep between sheets that smelt of myrtle.

★   ★   ★

Next morning she woke early and got out of bed, her toes searching blindly for her slippers. She wrapped herself in a thin dressing gown and headed for the bathroom next door. There was a brilliant freshness in the air. Downstairs she followed some dull clangs and other sounds and found Franca busy in the kitchen. The older woman looked up when Emma came in.

'Morning! May I call you Franca? I'm Emma.'

The older woman nodded and gave her a toothy smile.

'Can I have some coffee and a piece of toast or a bowl of cornflakes, if you have them? That's what I usually eat for breakfast every day.'

With some Italian muttering that Emma didn't understand, but which she guessed was clearly Franca's disapproval of such a meagre choice, she shuffled around opening various cupboards. She filled a tray with the requested items.

When it was ready, Emma asked her, 'Where can I eat? The dining room again?' She was so glad Franca understood English, otherwise things would have been more challenging.

Franca's voice was accented, but her English was good. 'Try the inner courtyard. That's where all the others go, although you're not likely to meet anyone. Leandro is already out somewhere; Marco came home in the early hours of the morning and we won't see him for a while.' She looked at the clock. 'And it's still too early for the Signora.'

Emma took her advice and went to the inner courtyard. It was blissfully quiet there and almost like a tropical garden. Large-leafed plants were planted in pots and borders, and the sound of water trickling from an ancient-looking fountain in the centre was almost musical.

Emma sighed in contentment. It was almost like being on holiday. She tarried longer than she intended to, merely because her surroundings were so special. She carried the tray back to the kitchen. 'Thank you, Franca. That was perfect!'

Franca shook her head. 'There is no need for you to carry your things back. It's my job.'

Emma tilted her head and smiled. 'I'm not officially part of the family. There is no reason you have to wait on me. I'll try and avoid it, if I can.'

★ ★ ★

Emma set to work. She parked the jeep next to the workshop and began to unload all the paraphernalia, and set up the lamps. There was a solid-looking used table on the side and she dragged it into the centre. It was a perfect worktable.

She'd been busy for some time before a long shadow spread across the floor to where she knelt unravelling a coil of electrical cables. Leandro stood in the doorway. He asked, 'Do you need any help?'

For some inexplicable reason, his appearance heightened her awareness in a way she'd never experienced with any man before. She scrambled to her feet and brushed the seat of her trousers. 'No, thanks! I prefer to sort things out on my own, to my own pattern. I don't work on outside jobs very often, so setting up is taking me longer than I expected. I prefer to work at headquarters. Maurice knows that and he gives me as many of those jobs as he can.' She explained, 'He rents a large warehouse. It's his office and a workshop. He relishes handling any outside commissions and enjoys working on the spot. He often comes back with new commissions from someone he's met while working on a job, because he's so affable and forthcoming. I'm afraid I sometimes get impatient with clients who look over my shoulder all the time. Maurice doesn't mind them. He enjoys talking and gossiping and it doesn't stop him working.'

A smile trembled on the edge of his lips. 'I see! Then I'll have to watch my step, won't I?' He stuck his hands into the pockets of his washed-out jeans and waited.

She coloured. 'I didn't mean it to sound like that. Of course, it's your privilege to check on progress when I'm working. I'm only talking about my personal attitude to constant time-consuming interruptions when I'd just prefer to work. Everyone, including me, expects an occasional chat, but I have had clients who kept me talking for half the day, and then complained because the restoration work took too long. Occasionally an employer has also tried to get too chummy, if you know what I mean. Sometimes I wondered if some men thought they'd bought me as well as the restoration work. That was annoying and embarrassing because we can't afford to be disagreeable to an employer, so I had to make them realize I wasn't interested without provoking them. It's probably why I like working at headquarters.' She smiled. 'I can tell the rest of the team to take a running jump if I like, and no one is offended.' She paused and considered him carefully. 'I don't think you're someone who wastes time, so I don't anticipate any of those difficulties with you.'

He looked around at the boxes and equipment and then caught her eye again. 'I hope not. I'd like us to get on. If anything bothers you, please tell me.'

She held his glance and nodded.

'I can see that your preparations are in full swing already. I was just about to have a mid-morning coffee with some of Franca's cake. Would you like to join me?'

His accompanying smile melted her reservations. She was tempted, but she declined. 'I don't want to get into bad habits, like taking coffee breaks all the time.'

'I can't imagine that you have any bad habits. You are too conscientious and polite.'

His dark eyes twinkled and Emma held her breath for a moment. Its effect on her almost made her lose her concentration for a second or two but she managed to sound natural. 'It wasn't exactly polite or customer-friendly to tell you I don't like being watched when I'm working. You could have resented that. Being perfectly honest is sometimes counter-productive.'

'I don't mind outspoken people. I'm like that myself. You noticed that yesterday. Somehow, I think we'll understand each other a lot better by the time you've finished your work here!' He lifted his hand and went on his way.

Emma stood for a moment and thought about him. Yesterday he'd been frosty and aloof when they met, but now that she realized how involved he was in the estate, she began to understand him better. Under his outer cover was a very pleasing character. He was an interesting man.

It got warmer as the day progressed. She could only imagine how warm it would be when the summer was in full swing. Franca passed the barn once and looked in briefly. She nodded and went on her way. Later she came back with some bottled water and some fresh orange juice.

When she'd finished unpacking and arranging everything, Emma went back to the house to view the paintings in the upstairs corridor again. There were paintings all along both the corridors. They weren't all valuable, but some were. Emma had no doubt that even the lesser-known paintings would fetch a decent price, if they were ever sold.

But somehow she didn't think that would happen. Leandro seemed determined to keep the estate intact in every sense of the word.

She decided to work on the most modern one first. The 'could-be' Dossi picture needed the most attention, but she wanted to show what she could achieve as fast as she could before she tackled that one. She lifted it from its position and carried it downstairs. She met Signora de Luca on the way, who glanced at the picture in Emma's arms. 'That has probably never left the upstairs corridor since someone bought it.'

Emma teased, 'Then it's getting a well-deserved holiday. A wellness holiday with lots of pandering and cosseting! When it's re-hung, I think it'll look a lot younger and revived.

Leandro's mother laughed softly. 'We all need rejuvenating from time to time, don't we? Have you had a mid-morning break? Are you hungry? If so, ask Franca for something. We usually skip a proper lunch. Everyone is busy during the day, but you are welcome to follow your own habits and timetable.'

'Thanks, but I don't normally have any lunch. I eat fruit if I get hungry. If I eat lunch here, as well as an evening meal, I'll go home looking like an inflated balloon.'

'Nonsense! You're very slim. Have you seen Leandro?'

'I saw him earlier on, on his way for a coffee break. I haven't seen him since.'

'Mariella phoned and wanted to talk to him.' She hastened to explain, 'Mariella is a friend of the family. Her father owns the neighbouring estate. Marco and Leandro have known her all their lives. She shares a passion for horses with Leandro. Marco is more interested in cars.'

Emma nodded silently and her brain refused to dwell too long on the information about Leandro and the unknown woman. It was none of her business. She lifted the picture. 'I'm going to get started. Is it safe to leave the picture in the shed overnight? I can take it with me to my room sometimes, but most of the time I'd prefer to leave it in a horizontal position to dry.'

'I think so. Ask Leandro when you see him.' She tidied some strands of hair that had escaped from one of her hair slides. 'Well, I must get on with my work too.'

Emma was too curious not to ask. 'Your work?'

'I do the book-keeping and the office work. Leandro can't do everything, and to be honest I quite enjoy it. If I didn't have something sensible to occupy my time for a few days a month, I'd end up like a porcelain figure in a corner cabinet.'

Emma smiled. 'I don't think so. You'd find something else to do. I'm sure your son is grateful for your help. It looks like he has plenty of other things to keep him busy.'

His mother regarded her with heightened awareness. 'Yes. More than enough. That's why I'm so glad he still enjoys riding. It gives him immense pleasure and it has nothing to do with estate work. He has several good friends, and plays golf now and then, but he always gives the estate priority over his private life.' She chuckled. 'Marco likes to pretend work doesn't exist.

5

Emma was satisfied with her first day's work. The workshop was a functioning unit, she'd examined the chosen painting closely, and she'd decided on a plan of action.

After the evening meal, she escaped as soon as it was politely possible. It was too early to go to bed and she went for a walk around the villa. She was tempted to wander further afield, but didn't. The surrounding countryside was still too unfamiliar and she might end up lost in the dark.

It was a wonderful star-lit night and after she came back, she drifted into the garden, ending up on an inviting stone bench hidden between some of the greenery. Grasping the edges of the seat, her imagination took her on a trip of fantasy. She thought about the generations of people who'd lived in the villa up to the present. She was startled when Leandro's voice cut in on her thoughts.

'Oh, it's you. I heard someone in here and I wondered if it was a fox. I thought you'd be in bed by now.' He sat down beside her without an invitation.

Emma smiled in the darkness. 'You were expecting to find a thief who comes to pinch your chickens when everyone is asleep?' He shifted slightly and they touched. She was intensely aware of him and tried to concentrate on the conversation and not on his physical nearness. What was the matter with her?

His voice held some laughter when he remarked, 'We don't have chickens anymore. One of our neighbours supplies us with all the eggs we need.'

She enjoyed the sound. 'To be honest, I was just sitting here and enjoying the evening. Even in the height of summer, I'm not able to sit outside in the UK very often in the evening. It cools down too fast. I was also thinking about your ancestors; all the people who've lived and worked here through the centuries. It must feel very strange to live where generations and generations of your family lived before you.'

He leaned back and stuck his long legs out in a straight line. 'I sometimes think about it too, but not very often. I just accept that I'm one of them and that I'm here now. When I moved back after my father's death it took me a while to accept this was going to be the rest of my life from then on.'

'No one forced you to, did they? I presume you simply felt it was your responsibility.'

Determinedly he said, 'Yes, that's right. My mother wanted me to carry on with my life and told me she'd muddle through with the help of workers, until I'd had more time to decide what I wanted to do. Marco was too young to get involved in that kind of decision at the time. I decided it was my responsibility no matter how much my mother tried to persuade me to take my time. I always intended to come back one day anyway. I might not have come home quite so soon, perhaps, but I always knew the estate would be my concern one day.'

She asked tentatively, 'What were you doing when your father died?'

'I was in London. On an exchange scholarship from my university. I was in the middle of doing my MA, but I broke off and came home.'

'And do you regret it very much?'

He leaned forward and folded his hands between his legs. 'No, not anymore. It did needle me for a time. But I now know this is where I belong. I enjoy the challenge of running the estate. I've seen enough elsewhere to make me realize how much this place, this region and the people mean to me.' He sat up and crossed his hands behind his head.

'It must have been very difficult for your mother, losing your father like that.'

'Yes, but she tried not to burden us

with her feelings after the funeral. I think she found it was very hard to accept because it was a car accident. If he'd died from a serious illness, she'd have had time to get used to the idea of losing him, and that might have been easier for her in the long run.'

She nodded to herself in the dark. 'What was he like?'

'Clever. A family man who put his family at the centre of everything he did. He was kind and quiet. He cared intensely about the estate.'

'He probably had the same kind of responsible feeling for it that you have now. Perhaps it's a feeling that's automatically generated in every new generation of de Lucas. Your ties to this land are infinitely stronger than an ordinary farmer who's growing what he needs just to survive.'

He shifted. 'You're probably right. What about you? I take it that you enjoy your work.'

'Yes, very much. I come from a small village, and everyone was flabbergasted when they heard I had decided to train as an art restorer. I think most of them have never been inside an art museum and they can't imagine what's involved. It meant moving away from home for my training, and I live in London now. Thankfully, my parents encouraged and supported me all the way.'

'What made you decide to be one in the first place?'

She chuckled. 'One day I watched a TV programme about what art restorers did. The idea grabbed me. I was always interested in art but knew I wasn't talented enough to be an artist. It seemed an excellent alternative. Most restorers hope to eventually find a job with a museum, because that's the safest and most permanent prospect. Businesses like Maurice's aren't so secure, because he has to find his own customers.'

'How many people does he employ in this team you talked about?'

She wrinkled her brow in the dark. 'Roger, Julie, me, and a trainee called

Stella. Maurice's wife does the office work, so I presume he has to pay her something. He needs a full order book, to pay all our wages every month.'

'Every business depends on good workers and good management.' He got up and stretched. 'It's time for me to go to bed.'

She looked up at his dark silhouette in the darkness. 'I'm going to enjoy it out here a little longer. Look at those stars! They're like diamonds in a velvet sky.'

He glanced up. 'I'll leave you to it. Good night, Emma.'

'Buonanotte! Good night.'

He wandered off and Emma listened to his shoes crunching on the pebbles as he went. The gate clanged as he shut it and she was alone again. She'd never felt so drawn to an employer like she was to him. Leandro de Luca was a multi-layered character. She'd seen how he could be distant, impersonal and almost churlish. She'd also seen another side of him; he was polite, open and friendly when you knew him better.

Perhaps her curiosity and interest in history had something to do with it all, and she also had a first-class fantasy. The atmosphere of the villa and of Tuscany were spinning a web of magic and excitement. She was here to work and Maurice planned to replace her as soon as possible. She reminded herself that she might be on her way home again in just a few short weeks.

★   ★   ★

Emma surveyed all the items she'd arranged on the table five minutes ago and went to search for a tool that must still be in the jeep. She noticed Marco emerging from the house dressed in jeans and looking fresh and spruce. He waved, and launched himself into the bucket seat of a red sports car. She waved back and wondered if he did anything around the estate. He seemed too unconcerned and carefree to be troubled with something as mundane as work. In film and books, Italian men were often portrayed as happy-go-lucky gigolos. From what she saw of him, Marco fitted that pattern very well, but Leandro didn't.

Emma concentrated on her work. She already knew the finished result would be impressive. She was surprised to hear voices in the courtyard and footsteps approaching from the direction of the house. Mixed up in the sounds was attractive laughter. Leandro knocked on the doorframe as he came in. A tall woman was at his heels.

He said, 'Morning, Emma! I hope you won't bite my head off for interrupting you for a minute. I wanted to show a friend of ours the picture. This is Mariella. Mariella, this is Emma.'

The two women eyed each other politely. Emma offered the newcomer a hesitant smile and said, 'Hello.'

Mariella acknowledged her with a nod. 'Hello. Leandro wanted me to see the painting before you start on it. I couldn't even remember which one he was talking about, even though the Villa Bella Rosa is a second home to me.'

Leandro added, 'My mother told me you'd brought the first one across and I was interested to see it out of its frame. Mariella said she was curious too, so she came with me.'

Emma gestured. 'Well there it is. It's much darker now than when it was painted. If you look at the canvas folded around the side of the frame, you'll get a rough idea of the original colours.' She couldn't help comparing the other woman's appearance to her own. Emma's spotted jeans, loose shirt, and ponytail lost the contest ignominiously. Mariella's riding outfit emphasised her slim hips to perfection. Her pristine white blouse was tucked into riding jodhpurs, and shiny black boots finalized a delightful picture. She had very attractive colouring, jet-black hair, a tanned complexion, and dark grey eyes.

Emma concentrated on explanations and cleared her throat. 'As far as I can tell, there aren't any obvious problems.

Once I've cleaned the surface dirt and the varnish, there'll be a distinct difference. Come and check it again when it's finished, then you'll see what I mean.'

Leandro studied it. 'It's strange to see it without a frame. It looks a lot smaller somehow.'

'I'm only planning to remove the surface dust today. Did your mother mention that I asked about whether it's safe to leave it here? I forgot to ask when we spoke yesterday.'

He nodded. 'Strangers seldom come up here. I'll give you the key of the shed if you like, but it'll be quite safe.'

Mariella looked around and slapped her riding whip against one of her gloves. 'It's going to be warm in here during the day.'

'Yes, I'll have to try to control the drying processes. It's bad for any surface if that happens too fast.'

Leandro offered, 'Remember about the windows. If you open them it will help.'

Emma looked towards the back wall. 'Oh, yes.'

Mariella glanced at her watch. 'Leandro, let's go. If we want to ride as far as the gully and be back in time for dinner, we ought to get going.'

With his eyes lingering on the canvas for a moment, he shared a brief smile with Emma, and turned away. Mariella was at his heels and her excited voice echoed as they walked around the corner to the stables. Emma wanted to ignore them, but her curiosity and something else she couldn't quite define made her follow their progress until turned the corner and were lost to sight. They seemed good friends.

6

Next morning Emma had been busy for a while and was now waiting for part of the surface to dry. She went across to ask Franca for coffee and then dragged one of the dilapidated chairs outside the shed to sit in the sunshine. She cradled the mug in her hands and closed her eyes.

'You look like a contented cat basking in the sun.'

Emma opened her eyes and met Leandro's. 'That's exactly how I feel.'

'It's nice to see you relaxing. You always seem very busy.'

She smiled. 'I have to co-ordinate the various processes sometimes. At present, I'm waiting for a particular section to dry before I carry on with the next.'

His gaze roved over her and appraised her lazily. 'I see. I'm going to the market to pick up something I ordered last week. If you're just filling in time, would you like to come? You'll probably enjoy a look around. It's the typical sort of market in this area.'

She didn't need to think twice. The prospect of spending time with him was exciting. 'Yes, if you give me five minutes to change into something that's clean and tidy.'

His eyes twinkled and he nodded. 'In the meantime, I'll check if Franca needs anything and meet you outside. In ten minutes?'

Emma locked the shed and hurried after him into the house. In five minutes she'd changed into a skirt and blouse and brushed her hair to hang loosely to her shoulders. She skipped down stairs and found him waiting outside in the car.

He gave her a reassuring smile and eyed her approvingly but didn't comment. He started the car and they drove off. There was an air about him that fascinated her, and she had to admit she simply enjoyed being with him.

Franca was dusting in the hallway. She came outside to shake the duster and she watched the car's progress with speculative, and approving, eyes.

* * *

On the way to the village Leandro said, 'Almost all the towns in Tuscany have a weekly market. Ours is nothing special, but local people still enjoy meeting and buying. The shops and supermarkets probably offer exactly the same products, but people still prefer to meet each other in the same way they have for centuries.'

It only took a matter of minutes to get there. The old houses dotted along the road were all steeped in history. Some stood in the middle of olive groves or vineyards; others populated the hilltops. Sometimes he pointed out some places of local interest near or far away on the horizon. They joined the congested traffic ploughing its way through the small village and merged with other cars as they pulled off the road to park in one of the fields.

He guided her towards the adjacent field, where dozens of trucks were standing in orderly lines. He gestured towards them with a wide sweep of his arm. 'This is our market.'

Emma saw the vendors had set up their shops in front of the trucks. They offered vegetables, cheeses, fruits and various other items of daily use. They meandered for a while among the gathering crowds and some people shouted greetings in Leandro's direction, or acknowledged him in some way as they went. She didn't notice their speculative looks.

Leandro stopped at one truck displaying a whole cooked pig. He remarked, 'This is a local speciality. You ought to try it. Would you like a porchetta sandwich?'

'As long as you don't expect me to eat a whole pig, yes!' She found it was quite delicious and he watched in amusement as she grappled with the sandwich and was ultimately forced to wipe away the juices from her mouth with his handkerchief.

Once appearances had been restored again, she followed him to the truck selling the item he'd ordered for the estate. After a jovial-sounding conversation with the stallholder, it was wrapped in newspaper. Leandro paid him and then tucked his purchase under his arm. They wandered along other rows selling shoes, clothes, cooking supplies, and various household things. It was like a supermarket on wheels.

The sound of Italians greeting friends and bargaining filled the air. Leandro stopped at a stall selling cheese and selected a couple of large pieces, explaining to the stallholder that he was buying them for Franca. The stallholder took care which piece he weighed and packed. Obviously, Franca's name carried a punch. The seller smiled at Emma and offered them some small samples. She tried them all. Leandro told her the man sold some of his cheeses to Harrods, and she could understand why. She managed to utter 'fantastico', which pleased him no end.

Leandro turned to her. 'I suggest we have coffee before we go home. There's a bistro just round the corner and they make great coffee.'

Feeling quite exhilarated by the relaxed atmosphere, she nodded. 'I'd like that.'

It was quieter, but the bistro was busy and they were glad to find a table in a shady recess at the back. Leandro ordered, the coffeemaker hissed, the waiter hurried back and forth; and then when the coffee came, it was really good.

Emma gestured towards their surroundings. 'Thanks for bringing me. The market was very interesting and unique.'

He leaned back. His light blue shirt and pale chinos complemented his bronzed arms and sunburned face. Emma realized her interest in him was growing at an alarming rate.

'I thought you might like it. These

days there's always a lot of cheap stuff and rubbish on the various stalls, but there are still a lot of genuine local products on offer too.'

She stirred her coffee. 'I noticed that one or two stalls sold herbs and spices. They also had packets of sunflower seeds. You harvest sunflowers, don't you? Do you sell your seeds?'

He shook his head. 'Not at markets. We sell our complete harvest to a wholesaler. We don't have anyone who's prepared to stand in the market all day. My mother would probably do it if I asked, but I won't. In the tourist centres the packets of seeds sell quite well, but we're too off-route for it to be worthwhile.'

'You could find someone who'd sell them for you, couldn't you? You only need cellophane bags, a pretty label and good fat seeds. It's not difficult to make labels with a computer. Even if you paid someone a small amount for each packet he sold, it might still be worth it.'

He tilted his head to the side, paused for a moment and then grinned. 'You're full of ideas, aren't you? But admittedly, it's something I've never considered doing for very long. On the other hand, anything that brings in money is worth thinking about. I know someone whose uncle has a stand in Siena, and he travels to different markets every day of the week.'

'There you are then! Ask him if he has room for a couple of packets, and have a trial run. I'll help you with the label, if you like. It would be fun.'

He laughed and the amusement in his brown eyes made her swallow hard. Emma looked down at the check tablecloth to hide her expression.

'Leandro! What are you doing here?'

Emma looked up and found Mariella standing in front of their table, with a dark-haired man at her side.

Leandro said, 'I came to pick up something from Alberto Morro, and I brought Emma along to show her our market.'

'So I see. Hello, Emma. This is my brother, Andrea.'

The young man smiled and nodded, and Emma responded likewise.

Mariella said, 'You're having coffee I see. Pity! I wanted to show you that saddle I want to buy. He won't be here next week.'

'Is he here? I didn't notice anyone selling horse tackle.'

'He's set up his truck at the rear of the church.'

Even though Emma appreciated the fact that they were talking in English for her benefit, she also felt uncomfortable with the thought she might be keeping Leandro from something that interested him. She said quickly, 'Please don't let me keep you. I can walk back to the villa. It isn't far. It won't take me long.'

Leandro lifted his hand to protest, but Mariella hurried to interrupt him. 'I'm sure Emma would be bored viewing saddles and horse gear, but there's no need for her to wait, or to walk home. Andrea can give Emma a lift back, and then you can come and give me your opinion about the saddle. You can take me home in your jeep later.'

Leandro looked at Emma and lifted his shoulders with a shrug. Emma rushed to reassure him. 'That's fine with me. If Andrea doesn't mind?'

Andrea smiled. 'Of course not. Our estate borders on Leandro's. It's on my way home and it will be a pleasure.'

Emma reached for her bag. 'That's settled then. It's about time I got back to work. As much as I enjoy it, I'm not here on holiday.' For a moment she didn't understand why she felt disappointed. Then she was honest enough to admit she was faintly jealous of Mariella.

Mariella smiled blithely. 'Good, that's settled then. Let's go, Leandro. Who knows who else may be interested? I just hope no one else wants it. I'm hoping I can persuade my father to buy it for me as a pre-dated birthday present, but I'd like you to see it first and then I'll ask him to reserve it for me, until I've talked my father round.'

Leandro commented, 'If it's first-class, it will probably be a pre-birthday and a pre-Christmas present.'

Mariella laughed and then turned away. Everyone hastened to join her. Outside, Mariella tucked her arm through Leandro's and said, 'See you later perhaps.'

Emma replied politely, 'Yes, bye!'

Leandro eyed Emma for a moment before he went with Mariella. Somehow Emma had the feeling he was also a little disappointed that their outing had ended abruptly, but perhaps she was only imagining things.

Andrea began to walk in the opposite direction and Emma fell into step with him until they reached his car.

His English wasn't as good as his sister's but it was good enough. He launched into a conversation about a friend of his who now lived in London. Emma made polite comments. It only took minutes until he dropped her outside the Villa Bella Rosa and left her there with a wave of his hand.

She went to check the painting and found she could now continue with the next section. She was tempted to just sit down and start working, but she'd ruined too many clothes by making similar impulsive moves. So instead, she went back to the house to change into her working togs.

As she worked, her thoughts wandered. She speculated whether the relationship between Leandro and Mariella was more than just amicable.

There was no reason why it shouldn't be. They came from neighbouring estates, they'd grown up together, they were similarly interested in horses and riding, and they came from the same cultural background. Emma wondered why the idea bothered her so much. She'd only been here a couple of days. She knew next to nothing about Leandro, and even less about Mariella.

7

The stable buildings were large. Emma passed them sometimes when she went for a walk behind the house after the evening meal. She wasn't certain how many horses were kept there but there were at least two, because whenever she passed, the same two looked at her with interest as they tossed their heads and waited for her to pat them. At first she'd been hesitant to go too near, because she knew nothing about horses and they looked intimidatingly large. But she soon realized they just wanted attention. Once she'd plucked up enough courage, they graciously allowed her to stroke their strong heads. They snorted their thanks and approval softly before she left them and went on.

The cobbled area in front of the stables was very clean and well cared for. Bales of hay were piled under the protection of the overhanging roof and a boxed-shaped enclosed area at the end contained the dirty hay and manure. She already knew that Franca's husband helped with the care of the horses, and noticed that Leandro seemed to spend a lot of his spare time there too.

He seemed to go riding often. She sometimes saw him astride his stallion looking like king of all he surveyed, and other times he took the other impressive-looking chestnut-coloured horse. Generally, he went off on his solitary rides when the sun was weaker and work on the estate had finished for the day, but sometimes he used one of them to ride to an outer field during the working day. Often Mariella rode across to join him on his evening rides, and Emma assumed that he called for her at her home sometimes in exactly the same way.

★   ★   ★

Walking towards the house after finishing work for the day, she heard a commotion coming from the direction of the stables. She rounded the corner to find Mariella kicking at a cat cowered against the wall. Emma had often seen the cat near the stable buildings. Mariella was shouting and raving in Italian at the tabby. Emma saw the rage in her face, and the cat was so frightened and confused that it cringed against the wall looking desperately for an escape route. It was an easy target for Mariella's boot. Emma rushed forward to grab the cat. It wasn't as grateful as it should have been. It lashed out and scratched Emma's arm before escaping from her arms to tear off round the next corner.

Mariella looked at her through hooded eyes. With amusement in her voice, she commented, 'Only an English woman would shield a stray cat.'

Feeling irritated, Emma retorted heatedly, 'Pity for dumb animals has nothing to do with nationality. You didn't need to kick it like that. It was scared to death. If you'd left it alone it would have scurried away of its own accord.'

She answered gruffly, 'I don't like stray cats or cats in general. It shouldn't be here. It's merely scrounging for food.'

'Cats are always looking for food. I don't think it's a stray either. I've often seen it around the stables and the other buildings. I've even seen Franca giving it scraps of food. I'm sure that if it wasn't welcome, Leandro or someone else would have driven it away a long time ago. It probably helps to keep the stables free of mice or rats.'

Mariella tossed her head and looked annoyed. 'Why make such a fuss about a cat, Emma? It's none of your concern.'

'It's a helpless animal and you were being unnecessarily cruel.' Emma didn't want to stir up Mariella's animosity, but she didn't intend to disregard things either.

Mariella stroked her hair out of her face and her eyes flashed. Her voice wasn't forgiving when she uttered, 'Don't you think you're making a mountain out of a molehill? You're only a visitor, a working visitor. Not everyone in this world likes cats. This is nothing to do with you.'

Emma held her glance. She didn't intend to give in. She liked animals, and there was no reason that she should take no notice of Mariella. 'That's true. But I don't like anyone being cruel to animals.' She couldn't help adding, 'Are you sure everyone would approve of your actions?'

Mariella laughed softly. 'They know me and I know them. You don't.' Her eyes were still guarded but she tried to sound more conciliatory. 'Let's not argue about something so trivial. Why don't you get on with your work, and I'll do what I came to do. I'm looking for Leandro. Have you seen him?'

Emma tried not to sound cross. Mariella had put her neatly in her place by reminding her she was here to work, and also that she should mind her own business. 'No, I haven't seen him all day.' She turned on her heel while saying, 'Perhaps you should ask someone in the house where he is.'

Still feeling livid, she left and instead of going towards the workshop, she went into the garden to sit down. It always seemed a little cooler among the greenery, and it helped to calm her anger. Perhaps she really was getting too worked up. She noticed she was beginning to dislike Mariella, and guessed that the feeling might be mutual. Emma still wasn't sorry that she'd tried to help the cat. The cat suddenly emerged from nowhere, and started weaving its way back and forth between her legs. It had left in panic but it was now showing its gratitude by recognizing its rescuer. Emma stroked its soft fur and she was glad she'd intervened. How could anyone be cruel to such a defenceless creature? It was time to stop thinking about it and get on with her work. The cat followed her to the workshop and then abandoned her to return to the stables once more. Mariella must have left.

Emma was still busy when Leandro knocked on the doorframe on his way back to the house. He looked at his watch. 'Hey, do you know what time it is?'

She checked. 'Oh, gosh! Time flies! I wanted to finish this section today, and I have. I was just starting to clear up.' She began screwing the lids onto the jars of the various cleaning liquids.

The afternoon sun was fading. Leandro took a close look at the picture. 'It's coming along really well. Even in this shed, with no extra lighting, the colours are already looking much brighter.'

She reached across the painting to pick up some stray brushes and cleaning cloths. He saw the scratches on her arm and fingered them with the tip of his finger. The gesture gave her goose pimples and was so unexpected that she almost jerked her arm away. She didn't, and then had to accept him holding it as he examined the scratches. 'How did this happen?'

'Oh, just some scratches the cat made.'

'What cat?'

'The one that lives round the stables.'

'It's normally very placid and it begs for attention. What did you do?'

Emma was silent and withdrew her arm and continued to put brushes into a nearby container with unsteady fingers. 'Nothing.' She didn't want to tell tales on Mariella. It might sound vindictive to his ears.

He didn't give up. 'I'll have to get rid of it, if it's causing trouble. We can't afford to have a deranged cat near the horses. Who knows what might happen.'

She replied uneasily, 'It isn't deranged. It wasn't doing any harm.'

'Then why did it scratch you?'

She decided she had no choice but to tell him. She did.

He looked reassuringly and smiled

softly. 'Oh, I see! I know that Mariella doesn't like cats; she never has. I don't expect she intended to hurt it badly.'

She said with easy defiance, 'That's not what it looked like to me. The cat was more or less trapped next to the wall and frightened. She didn't need to kick it like that. If she'd clapped her hands a couple of times, it would have disappeared of its own accord. I picked it up to put it out of her reach, and all the thanks I got for doing that are these scratches.'

He rewarded her with a smile, but its effect lessened when he said, 'Mariella is hot-headed and acts impulsively sometimes. People have likes and dislikes. She dislikes cats.' He let go of her arm.

She looked down and hid her expression. 'Perhaps, but I'll do the same if it happens again when I'm around. I don't understand why anyone has to be cruel without good reason. It wasn't doing her any harm, and it wasn't inside the stable buildings. I presume you and Enzo don't mind it being there.'

'No, it's harmless. I think Enzo feeds it scraps, and it sleeps in the stalls with the horses. They seem to get on together.'

'Then please tell Mariella that, and tell her to just ignore it if she sees it again.'

He gave her a soft laugh. 'That's asking for the impossible. When people dislike something, it never changes. Come over to the house and get Franca to give you some ointment. Have you had a tetanus injection?'

'Yes. I'll follow you as soon as I've finished clearing up.' She busied herself and turned away without waiting for a reply.

He considered her for a moment and could tell she was still annoyed about Mariella's actions. 'Okay. See you later then?'

'Yes, of course.' She listened to him leaving and felt slightly crestfallen. He'd stood up for Mariella more than she expected and hadn't admired her defence of the poor cat. Was that so surprising? Mariella was a childhood companion, and he knew about all her dislikes. Why did it matter what he thought, or that he hadn't understood her point of view?

Emma rang her best friend to tell her where she was, and why. Her friend was excited. 'Wow! How terrific, and Leandro sounds sumptuous.'

She was unaware of how much she'd mentioned him. She was still frustrated by his reaction to the cat rescue. 'Huh! I've met enough British aristocracy to destroy my faith in nobility generally. No wonder the French had a revolution and tried to eradicate them all.'

'I don't believe you. Your Italian marquis sounds delectable, and his brother sounds fun. Tell me about the house.'

'He is not my marquis and he has a local childhood sweetheart making eyes at him. I'm beginning to think she's beginning to object to my presence here. The villa is a big rambling place in wonderful surroundings. Absolutely breathtaking.'

'It's lucky that you broke up with Granville, isn't it? I saw him last week. He asked how you were. I think he hoped I'd say you were pining away without him. Is everyone else at the villa friendly?'

'Yes. No complaints. Next time you see him, tell him I've never felt better. I'm glad I noticed in time that he was a big mistake. He looked good and had the kind of background I thought was wonderful. It all fell apart when we seemed to spend every free minute with his family, or friends of his family. It was all an air-bubble of meaningless small talk.'

'Do you have to dress for dinner?'

'Sue! They're perfectly normal people. I don't turn up for meals in dungarees, but I don't need to impress anyone either.'

There was a sigh on the other end of the phone. 'It sounds wonderful, and two young Italian men every day into the bargain as well.'

'Don't let your romantic imagination run riot. I'll be back with you in London sooner than you think. Maurice wanted this job himself. He intended to lodge his wife somewhere locally and make it a working holiday.'

8

Next day when Emma went for dinner, Leandro wasn't there. Zarah explained he was playing golf with a good friend and they intended to share a meal afterwards.

Marco kept up a lively stream of conversation. Among other things, he told them about a friend of his who'd driven off the road into a ditch and ruined his car. Emma wondered how Zarah felt when she heard such things. Her husband had been killed in a car accident. She didn't comment, but Emma noticed her expression froze for a second or two.

The empty chair opposite drew Emma's eyes constantly.

When the meal ended, Marco insisted they all should drink a glass of Villa Bella Rosa's Chianti. 'Last year was one of our best ever.' He took a bottle from the sideboard and poured three glasses. Picking up his own glass, he said, 'Let's go outside.' He headed for the inner courtyard.

His mother shrugged. 'Shall we? If we don't, he'll come back for us.'

Emma laughed. 'Why not! I'm surprised he's still here and not out with a girlfriend.'

Zarah laughed softly. 'I've no doubt that he has plans. It's probably too early. Let's humour him for a while.'

The evening air was balmy and they settled on the thick-cushioned chairs in one of the nicest retreats Emma had ever known. There was birdsong around them and they sat watching the daylight fading. The atmosphere was almost perfect. If Leandro had been there it would have been perfect. Emma shook herself for thinking such thoughts.

Marco lifted his glass and the dark ruby colour shifted and glistened in the light from a candle in the centre of the table. 'To us!'

Emma repeated, 'To us! Cheers! Salute!'

Signora de Luca tapped Emma's glass. 'Salute, Emma! I'm Zarah.'

Pleased by the gesture of friendship, she touched the older woman's glass. 'Salute, Zarah!'

'Where are you going this evening, Marco?'

If Marco objected to his mother's questioning, he didn't show it. 'We're going to a new bar on the outskirts of Siena. Paolo and Antonio are picking me up. Paolo's girlfriend has volunteered to drive us there and she's bringing a friend.'

His mother nodded. 'And how will you come home?'

'In all probability, we'll share a taxi.'

She lifted her eyebrows. 'Then you have more money than sense! I'll have to tell Leandro to cut your spending money.'

'Don't give him ideas. I'll have to tell Mariella to distract him with other things.' He grinned in Emma's direction. 'I thought those two would have settled things ages ago. The biological clock is ticking and maybe Mariella is worrying about never having *bambini*.'

Zarah laughed. 'Don't be silly. Women have children much later these days. The other day I read about a sixty-year-old woman who had a baby.'

Marco leaned back. 'Wait and see. As soon as Leandro starts thinking about the next generation, he'll move like lightening. He knows I have no intention of settling down or providing the estate with heirs. When he mulls that over, he'll start to worry and look for a solution. He worries about everything.'

Zarah laughed. 'Marco, you are incorrigible. Don't be ridiculous. He's only thirty-three.'

'Apart from that girlfriend he had at university, and the occasional short-lived affairs he had when I tried to pair him off with someone, there's never been a real candidate, has there? And that's what life is all about. Love and passion!'

His chatter was entertaining, but

Emma also felt a little uncomfortable listening to family affairs. She wondered what life had in store for Leandro and the rest of them. She was glad that Marco and his mother were so relaxed and friendly when she was with them.

They went on to talk about a local family whose oldest daughter was getting married soon. Emma settled into the chair and listened. It sounded like there would be a massive celebration. Gradually, the wine glasses emptied.

She got up. 'The Chianti was wonderful. I'm now going to read for a while.'

Zarah looked at her watch and got up. 'It's bedtime for me.'

Marco squinted at his watch in the sparse moonlight. 'A book, Emma? At your age? Paolo will be here soon. Why don't you come with us? It'd increase my chances with other girls if I parade a beautiful English girl on my arm.'

Emma chuckled. 'Thanks for the compliment, but I'm sure that you're an expert in the art of attracting

93

fascinating girlfriends without any help from me. I have to get up early tomorrow morning.'

His mother laughed. 'One day he'll meet his match, and I hope it happens soon.'

They all parted in the hallway to go in different directions. Upstairs in her room, Emma looked out of the window across the Tuscan landscape at the twinkling lights of villages and towns in the far distance. There were shadows of swaying cypress trees casting their shadows along the roadways. This was a magic place, and no matter what happened, she was grateful that fate had brought her here for a while.

★   ★   ★

Next morning she was up and busy working long before the sun was at its hottest. She left the doors and the small rear window open. After mixing the correct ratios to make her cleaning liquid, she began on an outer edge of the painting with circling movements.

Emma heard steps and knew it was Leandro before he even reached the shed. He stood and watched her for a moment. With his hands in his pockets, he said, 'Morning, Emma! Everything okay? Are you always up this early?' There was a soft smile on his face.

She looked up and was grateful he couldn't tell how his deep voice was quickening her pulse rate. She smiled back at him and held his glance. 'Yes, I'm fine. It's no effort to get up early here. The mornings are so peaceful and beautiful.'

'You don't waste the morning, do you? Neither do I. We ought to share breakfast. I think Franca worries about you because she tells me you don't eat enough.'

Her colour deepened. 'Normally I never have time for leisurely breakfasts, except on the weekend. Did you enjoy yourself yesterday?'

He nodded. 'It's embarrassing. It seems I can't do anything or go anywhere without everyone in this house knowing about it.'

'You should do it more often; then no one would think it was so special. Where are you going now, or am I being too curious?'

'I'm off to check the progress of the sunflowers, and then I'm going to Greve to discuss business with the other members of our local wine conglomerate.'

'Do you sell your wine or sunflower oil at local markets?'

'No, but I've given your idea about the seeds some thought, and I might give it a try. I mentioned it to that man and he said he'd take them. Until now, we've always passed our sunflower and olive harvests in bulk to wholesalers, but it wouldn't mean much extra work to sort out a couple of sacks of good seeds. I'd just need to tip them through the right size sieve, check them over, and pack them.'

'The trouble with dealing with wholesalers is that they usually dictate the prices. You farmers should have a bigger say. You should persuade the other local farmers to band together and squeeze a bit more out of them.'

He laughed softly. 'You're a capitalist, aren't you?'

She coloured slightly. 'I don't know about that, but everyone is entitled to get as much as they can for what they produce. You work hard for what you earn.'

He hitched his hands onto his hips. 'I suppose it is a possibility. Perhaps I'll mention it at the next meeting.'

'Sunflowers are so lovely. It's amazing how they follow the path of the sun.'

'They only do that until they're mature and fully grown, then they stand still. If you monitor their progress properly you'll see that for yourself.'

'What are the seeds used for?'

'Producing sunflower oil that's used for therapeutic and cosmetic purposes, and of course for cooking. The seeds are also good for eating; Franca uses them in all kinds of recipes. They also end up in things like bird food sometimes.'

She nodded. 'I'm going to walk through your fields one day, and I'm going to take lots of pictures of your sunflowers before I leave.'

He watched her and tilted his head. 'I tend to forget their more beautiful aspects in my rush to make money. I'll see you later?'

'Yes. Till later!'

With a singleness of purpose, he strode off and left her to it.

★ ★ ★

A couple of hours later, Marco came to see her. He leaned against the door-frame eating a croissant. Bits of the flaky pastry floated to the floor as he sunk his teeth into the crunchy pastry liberally plastered with red jam.

'Good morning, *bella*! Hard at it, I see.'

Emma straightened and rested her

hands on her hips. 'Yes, since early this morning.'

'Leandro is up at dawn every day too.'

'He has to start early; presumably he needs plenty of time to cope with all the estate work. Perhaps he just doesn't need so much sleep. Some people don't. I know someone who only needs four hours a day.'

'Leandro should relax more. Life is too short to worry about money all the time.'

'A flourishing estate can only flourish if it's well-managed. Have you ever thought about the fact that he has no other choice?' She felt she knew him well enough to add, 'What do you do?'

He looked surprised. 'What do you mean?'

'I mean, what do you do to help him? Here on the estate.'

'Nothing in particular. I run errands, deliver stuff, that sort of thing.'

'But you spend money all the time; where does that come from?'

He cleaned the corner of his mouth with a finger and brushed some flakes from the front of his pale pink shirt. 'From the estate. I can take what I need, as long as it's within reason. I'm the younger brother, but I am entitled to some of the profits.'

Emma knew that at this moment her mum would dub him a spoiled, smooth operator. He didn't seem to feel uncomfortable or have any pangs of conscience that he was living off other people's efforts. Even though she liked him, she couldn't stop herself adding, 'You don't feel you should do more?'

His eyes blazed briefly and she could tell she'd touched a sensitive spot. 'I'm not idle or lazy, *bella*! I always help if someone asks me to. Leandro and I get on well. He knows he can count on me. One day Leandro will give me something permanent to keep me busy and I'll settle down here and do my bit.'

'Why wait until your brother suggests something? Tell him what you'd like to do.'

His eyes narrowed slightly and his smile was constrained. 'I'm enjoying life before I settle down to the serious stuff.'

'That's okay, but you still need to think about things from Leandro's standpoint. If you help him now, you'll reduce his workload and give him time to enjoy more of his life.'

He viewed her carefully and straightened. 'Know something, Emma? You have an angel's face and a keen tongue. I don't want to sound unfriendly but it's not your business, is it?'

She looked shamefaced. 'No. You're absolutely right. I apologize. It's nothing to do with me. Sometimes I forget myself.'

Marco's eyes twinkled. 'Ah! I don't mind, not really. Sometimes I actually enjoy being the black sheep of the family. It's fun. One day I'll have a fleece as white as snow. Promise!'

'I sincerely hope so.' She laughed.

'I'm going to Strada. Want to come?'

She shook her head. 'Too much to

do. Clear off, and try ensnaring yet another unsuspecting female in your web.'

He laughed. 'I will.' He added solemnly, 'I am grateful that I have a brother like Leandro.'

'You should be!'

He lifted his hand in farewell and a short time later, she heard his sports car tearing off down the driveway. She continued with her work without any more distractions.

* * *

A large crockery pot filled with huge yellow sunflowers met her eyes when she opened the workshop doors next morning. They glowed and glimmered. Their heads were the size of dinner plates and the seeds in their centres were arranged in a perfect geometrical shape. They looked magnificent.

She felt the heat rise to her face. Leandro must have put them there. She hadn't spoken of sunflowers to anyone else since her arrival. She brushed the surface of the silken petals and her thoughts were totally confused. He was serious, thoughtful and very busy, but he still found the time to make such unexpected kind gestures. As she worked, she glanced at the flowers now and then. They gave her a warm feeling inside.

*   *   *

At the end of the day, she left and locked the door before she went up to her room. After a shower and a rest on her bed, she leafed through Maurice's English-Italian dictionary and tried to remember the right words. She chose a summer dress in shades of green and white with wide shoulder straps and a swirling skirt. Descending the stairs, she came face to face with Leandro. She tried to recall what she'd rehearsed. '*Mille grazie per i girasoli.*'

He stared at her with a soft smile on his face. '*Con piacere, signorina!*'

Her cheeks were pink and her eyes unusually bright. 'It was very kind, and also unexpected.'

'When I was in the fields, I remembered you and thought you might like them. Are you on your way to dinner?'

'Yes.'

'Then we go in the same direction.' He followed her and leaned across to open the dining room door. The smell of lemon aftershave or shower gel wafted across to her as she walked past him. There was nothing she could do to prevent the tingling in her stomach. Emma warned herself not to focus on him so much. It would lead nowhere. But all her cautioning didn't stop her thinking he was one of the most attractive and nicest men she'd ever met.

9

When the weekend arrived, Emma decided she was entitled to some time off. Her work was going well, and she decided that she'd go to Florence for the day. It would probably be packed with tourists, but the chance was too good to miss.

Out of habit, she went to check the painting and was satisfied that it looked good. The section she'd already finished looked first-rate. She was locking the door when she heard children's voices. They were coming from behind the shed and going towards the main house. The boy was scuffing the ground, kicking up loose dirt, and looking grim.

Emma smiled at the little girl and received a shy smile in return. Emma said, 'Hello!'

Glad of a diversion, the little girl replied quickly in Italian but noticed

Emma didn't understand. A quick discussion with her brother ensued and then she surprised Emma when she said in English, 'Hello. Are you the lady who's doing the paintings?'

Extremely pretty, her jet-black hair was tied back in a bright blue ribbon; it cascaded to her shoulders and shone in the sunlight. Long black lashes framed dark blue eyes in a face with an even olive complexion. Her brother was dark too. He was older, taller, with bold questioning eyes. His expression told Emma that he thought unfamiliar women were a pain in the neck.

'Yes. I'm Emma.'

'I'm Alessa and this is my brother Antonio.' She tilted her head to the side and she looked at Emma with a puzzled expression. 'Are women good at repairing paintings?'

'Of course they are. Why not? Women can do most things men do, especially when they've had proper training. Where did you learn to speak such good English?'

'We go to an international school. In Rome.'

'Come on Alessa! Let's go and feed the goats.' Antonio reminded Emma of Leandro. He had the same dark eyes, high cheekbones, and strong chin.

Alessa pouted and she stood her ground. 'Don't boss me around! Just because you're older you think you can decide everything.'

Emma guessed they were very bored.

In a squeaky voice, Alessa explained, 'We wanted to go to the old cottage to see if we can find the gecko we saw last time we were there, but we're not allowed to go on our own, and no one has time to go with us!'

Emma thought briefly about her proposed trip. She liked children. 'I'll come with you, if you get permission. I'd like to see your cottage. I've been working all week and I haven't seen much of the estate.'

Alessa clapped her hands. 'Oh, really? Come on, Antonio. Let's ask Mum.'

Antonio grinned at Emma, all his

former reservations forgotten. 'That would be super!'

*   *   *

Antonio led the way, a few steps ahead of Alessa and Emma. The little girl skipped alongside, chattering. She clutched a paper bag with some bread and explained, 'I leave bread for the birds. I'm going to live there when I grow up and I like birds.'

Emma smiled. 'Then I understand why you are making friends with the birds already before you move in.'

Alessa giggled.

Emma liked the hilly contours of the landscape. The children led her up a gentle hill behind the house covered with ancient olive trees. From the top, she could see a lot more of the surrounding countryside. It was midday and the light was very beautiful. Tawny sunlight rippled across the scenery and interweaved between the olive trees nearby and the cypress trees in the distance. The air was clean and sharp; Emma took a deep breath. The hush was suddenly broken by the sound of hoof beats, and a rider on a big horse came hurtling up the slope from the other side.

Mariella reined in and studied them. She glanced at Emma and said something to the children in Italian. Emma admitted she was an extremely attractive woman, but there was something about Mariella that bothered her. Perhaps it was the way her dark eyes studied Emma too intensely. Perhaps it was her proud, almost arrogant bearing. Perhaps it had to do with Emma's recollection of her being cruel to the cat. Perhaps she was just being silly.

She talked to the children pointedly in Italian for a moment and ignored Emma; then Mariella explained in English, for Emma's benefit, 'I'm on my way to see their parents. They're at the villa, aren't they?'

Alessa answered, 'Yes. With Gran and the others.'

Emma looked away for a moment and for the first time she noticed the outlines of a small cottage in the hollow of a nearby field. The bright sun reflected from the windows at them like golden flames. When she looked at Mariella, there was also a halo of sunshine around her head. Emma wondered why the two isolated details made her feel edgy.

She felt the need to say something. 'The children want to show me their cottage.'

Antonio echoed, 'We're going to show Emma the cottage.'

Mariella looked towards the small building and nodded. She murmured something in Italian to the two children before giving her stallion the order to move on. She galloped off towards the villa without a backward glance.

Emma was relieved to be alone with the children again. The sun moved behind ancient olive trees as they went down the hill and crossed the field. The cottage windows were blank and lifeless again. She asked the children, 'Does Mariella live near here?'

Antonio indicated a nearby ridge. 'Over there.'

Her curiosity resolved, she said, 'Okay! Show me your cottage.'

Alessa set off at a run.

Looking around, Emma understood why Zarah didn't want her grandchildren to come here without company. It was a solitary place, hidden from sight and out of earshot.

It was a spartan building and looked neglected. The children showed her that there was a key under a stone next to the door. The windows had protective bars on the outside. The inner shutters were open at present. The children rushed inside looking for their gecko. Emma had a quick look inside and then sat down with her back against the knotted surface of a nearby tree. The silence, mixed with the children's voices, flowed around her. She listened to the children enjoying themselves as they talked excitedly and their feet pounded up and down the stairs. Eventually they came looking for her again.

She gave them some sweets she'd stuck in her pocket before they left and after another short excursion inside, they were ready to go home. She followed them as they skirted an adjoining field and returned by another route. Back at the Villa Bella Rosa, she followed them back into the welcome coolness of the house. They went in search of their parents and she went to look for Franca.

She was busy in the kitchen. She looked up when Emma came in.

'I wondered if it would be better if I leave the family to enjoy the evening meal on their own today.'

Franca shook her head. 'No, Leandro's sister knows you are here, and she wants to meet you. I just made some fresh coffee. Like some?'

'Yes, I'm thirsty.'

Franca gave her a mug. Franca's hands were age-spotted and she cradled her mug as she made herself comfortable. 'I heard you took the children for a walk. You like children?'

'Yes, I do. Although I've never had much to do with small children. Antonio and Alessa are nice kids and they wanted to show me their cottage.'

'Oh, that old place.'

Emma crossed her arms. 'The children think it's quite special. I can understand why. It's a life-sized doll's house. I enjoyed the walk and saw some of the surrounding countryside. It's wonderful.'

'Mariella came after you'd left. Rosella is older and they quarrelled a lot when they were children. I'm surprised she's so interested in meeting Rosella these days. She never made much of an effort when they were younger.'

'She rode past us on her way here.'

'Everyone wonders if they'll end up married . . . I don't. They're not suited.'

Emma swallowed a gulp of coffee.

'Leandro and Mariella?'

She nodded. 'And I don't think so just because Mariella made a big mistake when they were younger.'

Emma longed to know more, but didn't comment. It was none of her concern. 'Oh!'

Franca continued unasked anyway. 'They grew up together; neighbouring estates, similar ages — and everyone thought it would end up with lace and wedding bells one day. She always knew Leandro was a good catch, but she got impatient. Mariella has always had her head full of titles and money. I think she has an adding machine instead of a brain. When Leandro's father died unexpectedly and he was left to sort out the ensuing chaos, she suddenly realized that it might take years before Leandro would be in a worthwhile position.'

Emma tried to stem the flow. 'Franca, do you think you should tell me all this?'

Franca brushed her qualms aside.

'Why not? You're interested, aren't you? You know how much I care about the family. I'm not gossiping; I'm talking about Mariella.'

Emma coloured and laughed softly. Somehow she was almost glad that Franca didn't seem to like Mariella much.

Franca took a sip of coffee and continued. 'Mariella decided Leandro's prospects weren't so rosy, so she went hunting elsewhere. She has relations in Rome and she reckoned that in a cosmopolitan place like that she'd soon find what she was looking for. She almost angled a politician . . . almost, but not quite. We never saw him, but we know he was very rich, very influential and, unfortunately for Mariella, he was also clever. He saw through her, and realized that she was after his money and connections. He played her along for a while until he got bored and found someone else. Once he dropped her, and there were no other prospects in sight, she came back. By then, Leandro had sorted out the worst problems; and since then she's decided he isn't such a bad catch after all and she's trying her best again.'

Emma was uncomfortable listening to Franca, but the opportunity to satisfy her own curiosity was too great, so she remained silent.

'Leandro treats her like he always did. I don't know if he's aware of what happened in Rome or not, but there was plenty of gossip at the time. I think he knows exactly what went on. The Lorenzo estate borders this one. Mariella hasn't been able to steamroll him so far, and I don't think she ever will. I'd like to ask him what he thinks about her but I don't dare; he'd bite my head off. I think she's hoping that if she hangs around long enough, Leandro will take her, for lack of finding anyone else. Mariella thinks she'll angle him. She won't.'

'I'm not surprised that he'd bite your head off. Why should he lay his soul on the line? He's a grown man.' She picked up her mug from the table and took a sip.

Impatiently, Franca answered, 'I've known him almost since the day he was born. Most of the time I can guess what he's thinking.'

With tongue in cheek, Emma said, 'Then perhaps you should suggest he ought to find someone fast and get married and put an end to all the speculation.'

'I keep on telling him to settle down and get himself a family. He keeps telling me I'm an interfering old woman and I should mind my own business.'

Emma spluttered and laughed. 'I think he's old enough to sort his own life out, don't you?'

Franca nodded. 'There are plenty of local girls who'd jump at the chance of catching him. He's a good-looking man with character.'

'Perhaps he simply hasn't met the right one yet. It'll all fall into place one day I expect, and then you can plan the best wedding breakfast ever.'

'What do you think about him?'

Emma coloured at the question. She looked down. 'Me? He's very polite and intelligent, and I like the way he's met the challenge of keeping the estate going. I think a lot of men would have looked for an easier way out and built a life of their own, somewhere else.'

Franca's shoulders straightened. 'Not Leandro. He has too much de Luca blood in his veins. They don't give up easily. What about you? Have you a sweetheart waiting for you when you go home?'

Emma laughed. 'No, not anymore, and I'm not looking for anyone either.'

Franca got to her feet and put her empty mug down. She looked at the clock on the wall. 'It's time to start getting the evening meal ready. The meat is already in the oven.'

'Need any help? Your food is wonderful.'

Franca tut-tutted and gave her a toothy smile. She wasn't just household help; she was part of the family. She contributed to the well-being of the place in whatever way she could. Emma liked her. She was very down-to-earth. When they talked, Emma forgot completely that she was Italian and of another generation. Her English was very good, and her way of thinking was direct and very endearing. She reminded Emma of her own mother; whose favourite maxim was you should always call a spade a spade.

10

She hadn't had a lot of time to think about what to pack before she left London. That evening Emma chose her prettiest dress. If there was special company, she was going to look her best. It was cream, skimmed her figure, and complemented her hair and green eyes perfectly. She felt good when she joined the others gathered in the inner atrium, sharing a pre-dinner aperitif. Mariella, her brother and her father were also there. Andrea looked like his father. Mariella wore an elegant grey silk dress that rippled with every movement she made.

Leandro introduced Emma to the others. 'This is my sister Rosella, and her husband Stephano.' Emma shook hands and they gave her a friendly smile. 'And this is Pietro, Mariella's father.'

Pietro nodded and smiled at her.

'What would you like to drink?'

'Whatever you're drinking will be fine.'

Marco grinned and said, 'I'll get it, Leandro.'

Rosella's hair was dark and pinned into a smart chignon. Her clothes were deceptively simple, as well as chic and expensive.

Emma said, 'The children speak such good English. They told me they go to an international school? In Rome?'

Every mother liked talking about her children. She smiled at Emma again. 'Yes. Stephano is in the diplomatic corps. We're often posted abroad and so we think an international school is best for them. These days English is the second language wherever we go. It looks like we'll be posted to Helsinki soon.'

'That'll be a great contrast to your homeland.'

'Yes, I expect we'll miss the sun, but every country is new and interesting.

Have you been to Tuscany before?'

'No, I've never even been to Italy. I'm here to work, which doesn't leave me much time for visiting tourist attractions, but I hope to come back and see more of it one day. I think the scenery here in Tuscany is beautiful.'

Stephano added, 'You must find time to visit Florence and Siena. You can't work seven days a week!'

She laughed softly. 'Yes, I will try to visit them, but I have to restrict myself. My boss will start to complain if I spend time visiting places instead of finishing my work.'

Mariélla joined them, her glass in her hand. 'I expect Emma will be glad to get back to her friends and family. I know I would, if I had to work among strangers all the time.'

Emma couldn't resist. 'If all my clients were as friendly as the de Luca family have been, I think that I'd pester my boss to give me these kinds of assignments for the rest of my life.'

Franca interrupted them all. Wearing

a spotless white apron, she announced in Italian that dinner was ready and waiting.

They followed her into the dining room. The long table looked more festive than usual with white tablemats, a decorative white flower arrangement in the centre, tall crystal candlesticks, and silver cutlery.

Emma held back until the others had taken their place so she could figure out where she was supposed to sit. Mariella sat down next to Leandro, and his sister was on his other side.

There was an empty place between Stephano and Zarah de Luca. Emma talked to Stephano about some of the places he'd seen, and Zarah joined in. He knew London very well and the conversation flowed. She listened gladly; he was an interesting narrator.

During the meal, when Emma looked across the table, she had a chance to study Leandro and Mariella together. She was talking animatedly and trying to hold his attention. He sat tall and straight and his brows were drawn in a straight line as he listened politely and made appropriate comments. His black hair gleamed in the candlelight. Despite the fact that he'd never made the slightest effort to impress her, there was something about him that stimulated and electrified Emma whenever she saw him. Her reactions were juvenile. She wasn't a love-struck teenager admiring a beloved pop star.

After the meal, Emma didn't follow them back into the sitting room. She excused herself and reasoned they didn't see each other often and it was polite for her to leave them together without a stranger in their midst. Marco noticed she was edging away and tried to persuade her to stay but she refused. Hours later, she heard a car leaving. Presumably it was the Lorenzos. Emma thumped her pillow and eventually fell asleep.

Breakfast next day turned out to be a relaxed affair. Franca had laid the table in the inner courtyard as ever, and it was clearly intended that people come and go according to their own whims. Marco was just about to leave when she arrived. He was cramming a croissant into his mouth with one hand and drinking coffee with the other.

'Someone's in a hurry this morning.'

'I have a date. Someone I've been trying to persuade to go out with me for months. Very important!'

She laughed. 'One day you are going to get your come-uppance.'

He looked puzzled. 'What is that? Come-uppance?'

'You'll meet your match . . . You won't be in control of the situation anymore.'

'There isn't a woman alive who can control me! *Ciao, bella!*'

Marco put his empty cup on the windowsill and left looking as jaunty and cheerful as ever. No one else disturbed her breakfast. She thought about going to a tourist attraction today again. It was Sunday and Stefano was right, she ought to see something of the surrounding area while she was here. She'd check the progress of the painting and then decide where to go.

★ ★ ★

When she got to the shed, she met Leandro with the kids in tow. Her heart skipped a beat when she saw them. From the way he was fooling around with them, he clearly liked children. It gave her a peculiar feeling inside when she imagined what he would be like with children of his own. She uttered hurriedly, 'You're up early and already occupied, I see.'

He looked comfortable with himself in jeans and a checked shirt. 'You should have stayed last night. Why didn't you?'

'It was a family get-together. I don't suppose that happens very often anymore. I didn't want to interrupt.'

He watched her closely. 'I don't think you would ever get in the way. You're too considerate and polite for that.'

She was glad he thought kindly of her.

'I'm going to take the kids for a walk and give their parents some peace. Are you doing anything special? Would you like to come? I could show you a bit more of the place, if you're interested.'

She didn't hesitate. 'Um! I'd like that.'

He gave her a crooked smile that sent her pulse winging. She smiled back. They set off and walked past the stables and through the adjacent field. The children ran ahead and she fell into step at his side. It was a lovely day and her three-quarter white jeans and V-neck red top were perfect for the time of day.

Once they'd moved away from the house, he pointed at some distant places barely visible in the early-morning mist. They walked through fields of old olive trees and, although they looked dry and abandoned, Emma had no doubt that they produced olives en masse at the appropriate time of the year. After a while, the children ran ahead and started to throw a frisbee back and forth to each other. They were clearly enjoying themselves.

The tantalizing smell of Leandro's aftershave drifted across to her and mixed with her light floral perfume. It was so good to be out in the fresh air and to be with him. Her previous plans didn't matter anymore. They went on, and he pointed to the cottage down below.

She nodded. 'Yes, I went there yesterday with the children. I only had a quick look inside. They were hunting for a gecko.'

He laughed. 'Rosella, Marco, Mariella, Andrea, and I used to play there when we were growing up. No one has actually lived in the cottage for decades. It has outlived everyone's expectations, and strangely enough no one has even tried to break in or damage it, as far as I know.'

'It's fairly isolated. It's too far from the road for mischief-makers.'

'Youngsters get all kinds of strange

ideas these days because they're bored with life and looking for excitement.'

'It must have felt like having a real-life doll's house. You were lucky!

When they reached the cottage, Leandro found the key and opened the door. Emma stood for a moment and viewed the thick stone slates on the roof. They still protected the cottage from any stormy weather. Right now, with Leandro at her side, it was a romantic, isolated spot. There were two small dormer windows set into the eaves. Nettles and brambles rampaged next to the walls. It was silent around them, apart from the sound of some goats bleating nearby. Above her, a couple of wild birds were flying in an untidy formation. They flapped their wings in silent unison as they sailed across the azure sky.

The children rushed inside, chatting. Leandro motioned her to follow. There was a musty, unlived-in atmosphere in the rooms. The children hurried upstairs, their footsteps echoing on the planking.

Emma hovered in the boxed entrance area. One door opened into what must have been the kitchen, the second into what had most likely been a kind of living room, and the stairs were straight ahead. She crossed to one of the windows and struggled to wrench open the inner shutters. Someone must have closed them since she'd been here with the children.

Bright light flooded the room. Leandro looked round at everything with a slightly nostalgic expression. The room only contained pieces of discarded and damaged furniture. Looking out from one of the windows across the surrounding countryside, she looked towards the crest of the nearby hill.

She climbed the steep wooden stairs. The children were staring out of the unshuttered window and pointing out places they knew. She looked around briefly and then went back downstairs. Leandro was standing at one of the windows.

She said, 'It's a nice little cottage.' He

turned and smiled at her. Emma continued, 'It's safe and still in good condition.'

He shrugged. 'It seemed a very splendid place to me as a kid. We enjoyed being free to do as we liked here. We even slept here in the school holidays with sandwiches and candles. Today I just see the impracticability.'

'Children only see the adventure. They don't think it was built for people who lived here all their lives. It's hard to imagine how they managed in our modern world.' It was already quite warm outside, but much cooler inside. She looked at the solid walls and empty rooms. 'With care and a bit of imaginative decoration it could be attractive again.'

Leandro strode around closing the shutters. 'It'd cost a lot to make it habitable, and who's going to use it?'

'Your children perhaps? Or Marco's?'

He shouted up the steep staircase. 'Alessa . . . Antonio! We're going.'

The children's feet thundered down

the stairs and they ran straight outside. Leandro locked the door and deposited the key back under the large boulder again. Without a backward glance, he walked with the children to the edge of the next field of olive trees. Emma caught up with them and he pointed beyond the next incline. 'The fields of sunflowers start over there.'

The two children began to play frisbee again and Emma joined in. She enjoyed it almost as much as they did. The olive trees provided additional handicaps. Long wild grass spotted with poppies and small blue flowers that Emma didn't recognize grew around the trees. The children and she played for a while together, then Emma noticed Leandro was leaning against a tree watching them. She shouted, 'Don't be lazy — come and join us!'

He groaned artificially. 'I've had a busy week.'

'So have we. Me with my work, the children in school, you with your farm. That's no excuse.'

Alessa and Antonio chorused as one. 'Yes, come on!'

He straightened and came across. 'There's no peace for the wicked, is there?'

Emma wished her heartbeat didn't act so erratically whenever he was so close. He joined in and the children tried to out-trick him but they didn't succeed. Emma decided to try too. She succeeded in making him run more often but he understood the challenge and responded by making her run even more in return. It turned out to be a competition of the fittest. They didn't ignore the children and tempered the distances they threw for them, but they eyed each other with mischief in their eyes. Emma found herself moving automatically further away whenever it was his turn to throw, and hers to catch. She felt light-headed. He showed no mercy. She was forced one time to do a belly-flop through the grass because she was determined to catch the frisbee before it hit the ground. She dreaded to think about the effect of the grass on her white jeans. Leandro's laughter only made her more determined.

All of them were soon out of breath, but it was fun. Alessa and Antonio were reluctant to stop even when the adults were panting. They wandered further up the slope and were soon out of sight. They could hear them but couldn't see them among the rows of olive trees. Leandro sat down and plucked at a stalk of grass. He was in an exuberant mood.

Emma joined him. The silence around them and the field full of fragrant grass and wild flowers had a heady effect. She didn't trust herself to speak as her awareness of him grew. She tipped her face towards the sun and forced lightness into her voice when she said, 'This is wonderful. Just smell the grass and the clean air! Feel the sun on your skin.'

He laughed and looked at her indulgently. 'You are mad. You can smell clean air?'

The feeling of nearness and camaraderie was overwhelming and she cleared her throat, trying not to appear affected. 'Yes, I do. Perhaps you're not aware of it in the same way as I am because you live here all the year round. You'd understand me better if you'd spent more time living in cities. Then you'd know exactly what I mean.'

There was a flicker in his eyes and then they roamed her figure. He nodded. 'Yes, actually I think I do. I sometimes missed this place like crazy when I was at university. Probably for just that reason.'

She studied the familiar tanned face so close to hers and tried to assess his unreadable features. When their gaze met, her heart turned over. She lost any sensible thoughts and her sense of co-ordination. He seemed to make her boneless.

He threw away the blade of grass. The pupils of his eyes were dilated as he leaned towards her, leaving her no room to breathe. He did what she longed for him to do and kissed her in a lingering way that made her want more of him, much more.

Emma ceased functioning and his nearness kindled feelings of fire that made her senses spin. When he began to draw away, she longed to reach up and pull him back. She wanted him, more than anyone she'd ever known before. The emotions he roused in her succeeded in tying knots in her stomach. His kiss lasted seconds but for her, time stood still. They were both startled and the atmosphere between them was full of electricity. Leandro stared at her, his expression frozen.

He jumped to his feet in an effortless movement. He straightened abruptly, and unconsciously moved a step away from her before he uttered in an emotional tone, 'I'm sorry, I shouldn't have done that.'

Her breath was still too fast and her cheeks were too warm. She tried to control her visible longings and ignore the world-shaking effect of his kiss. Standing with his legs apart and looking down, the tension between them didn't lessen. She scrambled to her feet and found he was too close for her emotions to settle yet. 'It's okay!'

'No, it isn't. When you arrived, you mentioned that you'd had trouble with employers who tried to take advantage of the situation. That's what just happened. In a sense, I'm your boss. I assure you I didn't intend to exploit you in any way. I invited you to come for a walk without veiled intentions.'

Emma didn't like the idea that he might already regret that he'd kissed her. In this day and age, a kiss didn't mean anything to a lot of men. Clearly, his words told her he wasn't one of those. 'I don't feel led astray. In fact, I'm flattered.' She noticed that he was scowling at her, or at himself, and that helped to steady her nerves. Emma was aware of his clenched hands.

He said in a constrained voice and through tight lips, 'I'll get the children.

It's time for us to go back. Their parents are probably wondering where we are.'

He spun on his heel and left her feeling crestfallen and bewildered. She worried that an unexpected happening might now spoil their growing friendship. She wished she had the courage to tell him she had actually enjoyed it and wanted more.

Emma remembered as she trailed after him that he hadn't shown her a single field of sunflowers. They were almost over the crest of the field and in sight of the house. He'd also promised to show her some more of the estate. She watched him as he strode determinedly on and wished he wasn't so angry about kissing her. Perhaps he was promised to Mariella? She looked unseeingly towards the olive trees. She shook herself and carried on.

On the way back, the children's noisy chatter filled the silent gaps and forced Emma to concentrate on something other than this tall, dark man with his stiff expression. He and she didn't exchange a word during the journey back to the house and she began to feel mad at him. She wished increasingly that she could confess she was equally to blame. It was too late for that now; it was clear that he didn't want to talk about it or be reminded.

The silence continued between them when they entered the hallway. He called briskly to the children to follow him, and left her standing. Emma charged up the stairs feeling angry. She had the feeling they were in the middle of World War Three just because of a single kiss. She looked at her watch. It was still early. She didn't want to stay and face him any more today. She'd go off somewhere as she'd planned previously. She had no intention of facing his annoyed expression if they met. He'd calm down when he had time to realize that it was meaningless.

She changed her trousers, grabbed her satchel, told Franca she wouldn't be in for the evening meal, and hurried to her jeep. She drove away without a backward glance, and it wasn't until she was on the main road that she realized she hadn't thought about where she intended to go.

11

Leandro emerged from the house to see her Land Rover driving towards the main road. Why had he ruined things by kissing her? He guessed she wasn't the kind of woman who enjoyed flirting, or who took relationships lightly. He felt uncomfortable with himself.

She'd said she was flattered and she didn't seem to be annoyed, but he'd immediately felt angry with himself because he recalled how, on her arrival, she'd mentioned her dislike of employers who got too close. He didn't want her to think he was some kind of gigolo. The urge to kiss her just came over him and he'd enjoyed it for a few brief seconds and felt overwhelmed by the effect it had on him. Even recalling it now, he felt the intimacy of their kiss. It wakened hidden longings and yearnings.

He stuck his hands in his pockets. In one way he was glad he hadn't met her now, although it was only delaying what he'd intended. He wanted to assure her that he'd be careful not to step out of line again. She was too nice, too likeable, to leave her in any doubt about that.

He turned back and went into the house in search of the others. He needed to concentrate on something else.

*   *   *

Emma followed the main winding road to Greve. It was already hot, and as soon as she got to the small town she looked for a café with an outdoor table and ordered mineral water. There were lots of tourists milling about and she joined them as they walked the narrow streets. Emma was sorry she didn't have her camera. She concentrated on the town and what it had to offer, and tried hard to forget about Leandro's kiss, and his reactions.

The triangular town centre was ringed with shops and restaurants, and arcaded to provide shade from the sunshine. She bought a glass of Chianti and ordered a plate of pasta drenched in rich tomato sauce. She soon began to feel the effects of the sun and the wine, and sat watching tourists and the locals going about their business.

Two young Italians spotted her and tried flirting. After minutes of more sweet talk and flattery, they finally got the message and left her alone.

She finished her wine and wandered back to her car. The afternoon heat was strong and she was grateful for the wind that flowed over her from the open windows as she drove back in the direction of Villa Bella Rosa again. The forested countryside was dotted with vineyards, fields of sunflowers, and silver-leafed olive trees. She didn't intend to go home quite yet, but she went in that direction and looked for a spot to stop and loiter for a while. Numerous three-wheeled mini-trucks that seemed to be the favourite method of transport of Italian farmers, and various young Italians with their girl-friends' arms wrapped securely around their chests on their Vespas, whizzed past.

Emma came to the crest of a gentle hill and pulled into a narrow siding. Under the shade of a tree, she looked across the sea of golden sunflowers in a nearby field. She was tempted to get out and wander through them, but she didn't. Instead she sat staring ahead. She wished Leandro hadn't kissed her. It had changed everything. She was also honest enough to admit she'd loved it, and the memory of its effects made her wonder how it would feel to be really loved by him. It had wakened devils inside her, and she had never physically wanted a man as badly as she did him at that moment. The physical need was instant, but he attracted her in other ways too.

There was no point in worrying about his behaviour afterwards. There could be all kinds of reasons. Perhaps he'd given Mariella some kind of a promise; perhaps he didn't want to complicate their business association; perhaps she wasn't socially suitable in his eyes; perhaps he intended to marry someone rich; or perhaps he just wanted an Italian wife. There could be dozens of reasons. She must stop thinking about him.

She fumbled in the glove compartment looking for a paperback, then settled down to read. Although it was hard to concentrate at first, she forced herself to do so. By the time she finished the story, she had the satisfaction of knowing she'd already guessed who did it. The sun was a golden haze above her and sending an apricot glow across the fields, towns and villages. Emma felt like a dreamer, out of touch with reality as she viewed the scene. Tuscany weaved its magic on her and she accepted it gladly. She checked her watch. It was time for the evening meal at the villa. She could return now and slip upstairs again.

Starting the engine and straightening her shoulders, she reminded herself she had a job to do, and she'd do it until Maurice came to replace her, or until she'd finished the work herself. The first picture was almost ready, and she was pleased with the result. She'd brought out the original colours again and the relining of the canvas would stabilize it, and help to extend its lifespan.

* * *

It was getting dark when Emma reached the villa. The air was still balmy. She hoped Leandro didn't realize it was his fault that she'd scuttled off for the day. She went straight to the garden and sat in her secluded spot under the covered archway. The heavens were star-spangled, and scents from the flowers in the garden wafted in drifts of perfume around her. Who would willingly exchange something like this for a life in the city?

'Can't sleep?' Leandro's voice, deep and sensual, sent a wave of awareness through her.

For a moment she had to catch her breath, before saying as casually as she could, 'I haven't tried yet. I've been to Greve. I only just got back.'

He sat down next to her on the bench and was so close it left her no place to breathe. He stretched his long legs and his thigh touched hers. Her mind and body were frozen.

'Did you like it?'

'It was very picturesque, and I enjoyed it until a couple of flirting Italians tried to chat me up!'

He winced as he thought about what had happened between them that morning. 'You missed the evening meal, but I expect Franca has something if you're hungry.'

'I ate a delicious plate of pasta and tomato sauce in Greve. I'm still full up.'

There was a moment's silence. Then

he said, 'I didn't intend to take advantage of you this morning, Emma. I remember very well how you told me about employers who bothered you in the past. I'm your present employer and I didn't set out with the intention of making you feel uncomfortable, honestly.'

She looked down at her hands. 'It's okay! I tried to tell you that earlier on. It wasn't a one-way thing. I was perfectly capable of feigning apathy, but I didn't, did I?'

'I've been aware of how attractive you are ever since you arrived, but that's no excuse for ignoring the rules of respect and courtesy towards someone who is working under my roof.'

She stared into the darkness. 'I wasn't insulted, Leandro. It was a compliment.'

'Good. I'm glad you're not too disappointed in me. I wanted to clear the air between us. I didn't feel happy about what happened when I started to think logically.'

'Don't give it another thought.' She looked up at the sky. 'It's lovely here, but I think it's time to go to bed.'

He seemed almost glad to get a signal that it was time to go. He got up. 'Yes, you're right. We both have a busy day tomorrow. Good night, Emma.'

'Good night.'

He strode off into the darkness and she was just relieved that they were on speaking terms again. Her mood slowly spiralled upwards again.

12

Emma decided she had to adjust her working times. It was better for the paintings if she worked at the coolest time of the day. She'd set her alarm and got up earlier. Not all drying processes benefited from fast drying.

She'd been busy for a couple of hours with a short break for coffee and a bite to eat, when a soft knock on the framework made her look up. It was Leandro. A wave of delicate pink flowed over her face.

'Can I disturb you for a minute?'

She met his glance. 'Yes, of course. Can I help?'

'As a neutral person who's observed the family closely for a while, I'm interested in what you think about me involving Marco in estate work.' He ran his hand through his hair. 'You seem to have jogged his conscience a bit, and recently he even asked me to give him something worthwhile to do.'

His eyes shone in the semi-darkness. He moved around the table and picked up one of the brushes. He played with it as he talked. 'Marco is almost nine years younger, and he was still in school when my father died, so it was up to me when I came back. I muddled through for a while until I gradually began to understand what was needed to keep the estate going. If Marco did take some part of the work off me, it would be great. Do you think it would be good for him, me and the estate?' He gazed at her intently.

Why was he asking her something so personal? Her mouth was dry. She was flattered, but why did he want her to judge the situation? 'I can't say what's right or wrong for you, or for Marco. I don't know the two of you well enough for that, but I do think he's very capable of doing a lot more than you think he is. You and your mother tend to treat him like a spoiled child who's still growing up, so he acts like one, because it's easier and more fun.'

His eyebrows lifted and his initial expression was one of surprise and then of measured agreement. He nodded.

Emma continued, 'It's none of my business, but I think it's time he learned that life isn't just one long party and that he has to take his share of the responsibilities if he expects to draw on the financial rewards. I suspect that deep down he's bored and that's why he spends so much time chasing girls all the time. Give him a job and make him accountable for it. If you do, don't interfere thereafter, even if he makes mistakes. People learn fastest from their mistakes.'

His eyes twinkled and he threw back his head and laughed. 'For someone who doesn't want to get involved, you certainly have fixed ideas. What makes you think it would be the right solution?'

She coloured. 'My brother was a bit like Marco. He didn't chase girls all the time. Well, not as intensely as Marco does, but he was mad about rugby, and everything else took a back seat. My father defended him and kept on saying he'd grow up one day. I'm glad that my mother eventually put her foot down and gave them both an ultimatum. Either they got their priorities right, or she'd move out and leave them to it.'

'What does your father do?'

'He has a small-holding, producing bio-vegetables. It doesn't make a great deal of money, but they have a decent lifestyle. Dad was intimidated by Mum's threat — they've been married for over thirty years. He caved in right away.' Leandro's mouth twitched. 'Darren came round gradually after she insisted she'd cut his financial support if he didn't work regular hours for it. He works alongside my father now. He wouldn't admit it, but I think he actually likes the work. He's outdoors all the time, he can arrange his working hours to suit himself, he has a regular pay packet, and he feels he's doing something worthwhile.

Bio-farming impresses country girls no end. He got engaged recently to a very nice girl who is daft enough to stand on the sidelines every time he plays rugby.'

He laughed. 'So you're a farmer's daughter? Who would have thought it? I can't imagine you on a farm.'

She relished the hidden compliment. 'Why not? Just because I wanted to do something different?'

With his tongue in his cheek, he commented, 'It looks like people should reckon with the women in your family.'

'That's true! My gran is also a bit of a hothead.'

'And you now hate vegetable farming and farming in general?'

'No, of course not. I'm a dab hand with a tractor, and I don't mind mucking in when I'm home and they need help with harvesting.' She gave him a smile.

He paused before he asked, 'And . . . do you have a special boyfriend?'

She shook her head and said, 'I've never met anyone I felt so strongly about. I broke up with my last boyfriend just before I came here, and I don't miss him at all. He was wrapped up in his upper-class family and career prospects. He got tetchy if I didn't show enough interest in the spreadsheets he made about his finances, and he updated them constantly.' He laughed and nodded. 'Everyone needs to think about the future, but when you're thirty, you should be planning to have some fun along the way before you start worrying about your pension. Who knows if you'll even get that far? A bus could run over you tomorrow, and all your contributions go up in smoke.' She paused and eyed him carefully. 'You don't seem to have much time for your own pleasures, do you? That's another very good reason to let Marco take some of the load.'

He chuckled and was then silent for a moment. 'You're quite a special person, Emma. I'm glad we're friends — good friends, I hope.' Unexpectedly he offered her his hand and she took it. He held it a mite too long, but she didn't notice; she was lost just looking at him. She wanted more and looked longingly at his lips.

He nodded and then studied the picture lying flat on the table. 'That is looking good. Almost like it's newly painted.'

'I'll be able to re-hang it in a day or so.'

'I'm sure my mother will be delighted when she sees it. She was sceptical about the extra cost, but sometimes you have to throw caution to the wind, don't you?'

'Exactly! If you hadn't decided to do something about the pictures, they'd have degenerated further and made restoration more difficult. Give Marco something to do; it will be the making of him.' She paused and looked at her watch. 'I have to contact Maurice. He wants some before-and-after pictures. Perhaps he'll stop sending me constant instructions and unasked-for advice when he sees I'm managing without him.'

'When I think of all the pictures in this place, you'd have a lifetime of work, if I could afford to keep you employed.'

Emma imagined a lifetime here with him, and a shiver went down her spine.

As he strolled out, he waved farewell over his shoulder. The light from outside flowed into the shed together with the scent from the pots of geraniums standing against the walls in the sun. He closed the door behind him. It was much darker again and she wished he'd stayed longer. She glanced up at the sunflowers and even though the heads were drooping, they still delighted her because they'd come from him. Emma tried to be sensible and hoped he hadn't noticed how much she liked him. She needed to keep her feelings under control and hide her emotions whenever he was near. He wasn't looking for affection or love. If she couldn't have that, she'd accept friendship.

No man had ever had such a deep

and lasting effect on her before. He could do what he liked, say what he liked; nothing lessened her attraction to him. Something clicked in her brain and Emma realized she had fallen in love at last — with Leandro de Luca. Why him? She gripped the edge of the table and the knowledge left her reeling for a moment. It was wonderful to admit it, even though she also knew there was no chance for romance between them. She felt vibrant and alive when he was around, and had a feeling of emptiness when he left.

13

Next day footsteps heralded the appearance of Leandro, his mother, Franca, and Mariella.

Leandro ducked his head and came in. 'We won't bother you for long, but I wanted to show my mother what the first picture looks like. It's almost ready, isn't it?'

Emma nodded. She was apprehensive. Her restoration and cleaning had brought out colours that had been hidden by decades of dirt and ageing varnish. They all crowded round the table where the painting lay flat on the surface. She hadn't yet put it back into its frame. They all looked at it in silence for a couple of seconds.

Then Zarah de Luca said, 'It's lovely! I never thought it had so many colours. Look at that red curtain and the dark green pot on the table. They were almost black before Emma started.' Emma sighed inwardly with relief.

Mariella circled the desk. She said, 'Yes, I see what you mean. Who'd have thought it could look so good?'

Emma didn't know if she should add a comment or not. In the end, she remained silent and waited. Leandro was at Mariella's shoulder.

Mariella looked up at him affectionately and continued, 'Surprising what can be achieved, isn't it?' Leandro returned Mariella's smile, and for a stupid moment Emma felt very resentful. Mariella reached out towards the table, and the painting.

Emma hastened to stop her. 'Please don't touch it. I want to give it a couple more days to be certain that the surface is really hard. At the moment any kind of pressure could still distort the brushwork, even though it seems okay.'

Mariella nodded and Emma could see she was hiding her irritation. She'd seen enough and turned to Leandro. 'I came deliberately near lunchtime because

I hoped I could share lunch. I haven't seen you or your mother for ages.'

Leandro was still looking at the picture. 'That's not true and you know it, but you're welcome to join us; you know that. Franca always has something on the stove.'

Mariella's laugh tinkled. 'That's good. Let's go across then, before you find something more urgent to do and disappear again.'

'I planned to check the vines in the upper field this morning, but I may as well stop for a break now. What about you, Emma? Join us; make an exception for once.' He smiled at her and Emma was tempted.

'No, thanks! I'd like to finish cleaning the frame before it gets too hot. Another time, perhaps?' He studied her face for a moment before he nodded silently.

Zarah touched her arm. 'You've done a wonderful job, Emma. Now I understand better why Leandro thought it was important to look after the paintings.'

They left and Emma closed the door after them to prevent unnecessary dust settling anywhere. She turned her attention to finish preparing the frame. She thought about the next painting. She'd fetch it down to the shed and take a closer look this afternoon.

★   ★   ★

The following weekend, she was surprised when the children invaded the shed.

'Emma, we're going on an outing to the beach tomorrow.'

Emma looked up and continued to make circling movements with a soft cleaning pad across a section of the second painting. 'Are you? That's good. I expect you'll have a great time. I used to love outings to the seaside.'

Alessa nodded. 'Will you come with us?'

She looked up at the little girl's animated expression. 'It's very kind of you to think of me, Alessa, but it's a family outing. You come and tell me all about it afterwards.'

A darker figure filled the open doorway and Leandro said, 'If you'd like to come, we'll be pleased to have you along. We promised Alessa and Antonio we'd take them when they were here last weekend. My sister and brother-in-law are invited to some high-class celebration this evening, so the children are with us for the weekend. We've some really lovely beaches within travelling distance.'

Confused by the sudden invitation, Emma's throat was dry and colour rushed to her face when she met his eyes. 'Actually, I was planning to hang the first painting tomorrow and then carry on with this second one.'

He made a clicking sound with his tongue and shook his head. 'Franca will skin you alive if you work on a Sunday.'

'Oh! Yes, it's Sunday. I'd forgotten.'

'Franca is a strict Catholic. She hasn't missed high mass on Sunday as long as I can remember. According to

Franca, no one should work on Sunday. Be warned! I have the devil's own job to persuade her that I have to work during harvest time.'

'Why doesn't she doesn't object to you going on family outings?'

'Because that's not work. Would you like to come, or would you prefer to relax in the bath with a book, like my sister used to do?'

Alessa joined in, 'Do come, Emma. It will be fun.'

Emma looked at her and smiled. 'Who can resist? All right, I'll come.'

Alessa clapped her hands. Leandro smiled.

'My mother is coming too and Marco, if he can get out of bed on time. I thought we'd leave after breakfast and make a day of it. Rosella intends to pick the children up on Monday morning. She's had special permission to keep them out of school for a day, but they have to be back on Tuesday morning without fail.' Alessa groaned. 'Franca will provide us with a picnic.'

His smile had a silly, wonderful effect on her and she was exhilarated by the idea of spending a whole day with him. 'Right. I'll be ready whenever you are.'

Alessa shouted 'Hurrah!' and Leandro smiled before he turned and disappeared.

Emma felt extra pleasure as she thought about the prospect and was fully motivated as she went on working until late that day.

★　★　★

When everyone was gathered around the table for the evening meal, the children were also there. They provided a lot more noise, jollity and excitement. Zarah de Luca tried in vain to dampen their spirits. Alessa prattled on continuously about tomorrow's trip, and Antonio joined in now and then too.

Leandro eyed Emma across the table and shrugged his shoulders before he warned the children, 'Don't forget, no running off on your own, no climbing up crumbling rock faces, and no back-talk when you are told to do something, okay? If you play us up, we won't take you again and we'll tell your mother that you behaved badly.'

The children knew he was teasing them.

Antonio asked, 'What about Emma? Does she have to do as she's told?'

Tongue in cheek, Leandro said, 'Of course! I'm the boss.'

Antonio studied Emma. 'I think she's likely to cause more trouble than we do. She's not used to being bossed around — she's her own boss.'

Leandro and his mother laughed and looked at Emma. He said, 'He's figured you out. I think Antonio may be right, but I'm willing to take the chance.'

14

Emma didn't have a swimsuit; she'd forgotten to pack one. She did have shorts and a T-shirt, and that was what she wore. Her legs were pale, but they were shapely and long. She took more time than usual to get ready and avoided asking herself why. When she heard the children's excited voices outside, she picked up her backpack and hurried downstairs. The children were waiting eagerly near Leandro's mini-van.

Alessa was skipping around in circles. 'Uncle Leandro is fetching the picnic basket.'

Zarah was already there and smiled at her before she loaded some things into the boot. 'Morning, Emma! The children have been running round in circles for hours.'

Leandro joined them with a bulky

basket. 'I think Franca has packed enough for a week.' He smiled at her.

Emma's pulse increased and she returned his smile. 'She probably can't bear the idea of anyone going hungry.'

He put the basket into the boot and looked at Antonio and Alessa. 'You two, in the back; Emma, in the middle; and you can sit in the front, Mum, to make sure I'm on the right road.' Emma got in and fastened the belt.

By the time they reached the main road, Antonio was already clicking away on his Nintendo. Emma looked out of the window and listened as Leandro and his mother pointed out things along the route. There was soft music on the radio and Emma concentrated on enjoying the journey; it gave her a chance to see some more of the local countryside. Leandro glanced at her sometimes in the mirror and when their eyes met Emma reminded herself that she shouldn't be fantasizing about a man she hadn't known existed until a few weeks ago. For all she knew, he might be Mariella Lorenzo's serious boyfriend. He was her employer — but it didn't stop her studying his face and dreaming about his lips.

They reached the coast an hour and a half later. Leandro had chosen a beautiful beach. It curved in a lazy arc and it had soft golden sand. Antonio promptly put his Nintendo away when he realized they'd arrived. He and Alessa couldn't wait to get out of the car. Leandro gave the children some playthings to carry. They hurtled down the steps that were cut into the rocks.

He, Emma and his mother shared the rest of the things. It was already hot and the sun was shining. In a few weeks the beach would always be packed with tourists, but today the sands were only nicely populated.

Leandro suggested that they spread their picnic-rugs near a grass-covered incline below the rock face. It was further away from the sea, but more sheltered from the sea breezes. The children longed to tear off towards the ocean right away but Leandro held them back and insisted they wait until someone could go with them. They filled the time impatiently by scrabbling about in nearby rock pools, looking for crabs.

Watching them, Leandro explained, 'It's too risky to leave them on their own. We're too far away to control them from here. If they got into trouble, it might be too late by the time I reached them. There are strong currents further out, and even though you tell them to stay close to the shore, you can never be sure children will listen.'

His mother nodded. 'I'd never forgive myself if something happened to them.'

Emma added understandingly, 'We can take it in turns to go with them if they want to spend a lot of time in the sea, but I expect they'll be happy to play around here near us once the first excitement has worn off.'

Leandro was divesting himself of his chinos and polo shirt. He wore swim shorts in bright Hawaiian colours and looked good; his long legs were brown and firm, and his body was wide-shouldered. The physical work on the estate merely increased the bodily attraction of a man who was already eye-catching. The sea breezes played with his hair and he pushed at it impatiently. He called to the children. 'Hey, ready?' Antonio and Alessa needed no second invitation. He looked at Emma. 'Coming?

Emma shook her head. 'I haven't brought a swimsuit with me. I don't mind. I'll stay and guard everything.' She told his mother, 'Why don't you go with them, Zarah?'

Leandro didn't argue with her. He removed his watch and gave it to her with a smile before he ran after the children, who were already on the move. With his long strides he soon caught up with them, and Emma heard the children squealing as a race ensued to see who'd reach the water first. His mother was wearing Bermuda shorts, a straw hat and a colourful top. She followed them at a slower pace with her camera.

They were gone for a while. Emma

hugged Leandro's watch and saw their diminutive figures having fun near the water. When they came back Leandro flopped down beside her, grabbed a towel and began to dry himself. Seawater was trickling down his face and Emma wished she could reach out and touch him. She busied herself, helping the children to dry off. They then wanted something to eat. Emma proceeded to search the plastic containers. By the time Zarah joined them they were already munching away.

Zarah smiled. 'We've just arrived, and look at that. We've already captured two hungry sea lions.'

A voice at Emma's side said, 'Three! Can I have a sandwich too?' Emma held out the plastic container and Leandro took two.

Alessa and Antonio picked up their buckets and spades and set to work creating a sandcastle. It began with a small inner keep with strong defences; then the inner walls were strengthened, towers added, outer walls created, and finally a moat and a drawbridge constructed with seawater and pieces of wood. The adults watched them and relaxed. The wind was blustery but not unpleasant. It plastered Emma's T-shirt to her body and messed her hair, but she loved the smell of the salty air and the feeling of sand under her bare feet.

Up above, seabirds called noisily to each other and circled in the blue heaven. Most of all she loved being with Leandro. He seemed to be enjoying himself, so everything was perfect.

His mother looked at her grand-children and then got up. 'I think I'll join them. They need someone to show interest and support, otherwise they'll just get bored and start to grumble.'

Leandro turned to Emma. His near-ness set her pulses racing. He asked, 'What do you think of it?'

'The beach?' She replied honestly, 'It's lovely.'

'If you'd like to swim, there's sure to be a shop nearby where you could buy a costume.'

Emma pushed her wind-tossed curls out of her face. 'No, I'm not keen on swimming. Don't worry; I'm enjoying myself.'

'Most people love swimming. Why don't you?'

Staring straight ahead, she answered, 'I learned how to swim in school. The first couple of lessons were okay, but our teacher had over twenty kids to watch. One day our classroom bully pushed me in, down the deep end of the pool, and even though the instructor noticed in time, it put the fear of god into me. I've never lost the fear of deep water since then. I thought it would disappear in time, but it hasn't. These days I never swim beyond my depth and I'm not very bothered if I never swim.'

Leandro's eyes followed how the children and his mother were widening the castle's moat. He was silent.

She ploughed on, giving him a shaky smile. 'I've often wondered if I'd panic on a sinking ship. But perhaps under those circumstances the primitive urge for survival everyone has buried inside them would automatically kick in.'

Before she realized it, he reached across and covered her hands with his. His gaze was disconcerting. 'I understand why you feel frightened. Ever thought about getting professional help?'

'You mean some kind of therapy? No. I always presumed the fear would disappear one day.'

'What about the boy? Was he punished?'

'Oh, he was banned from any more lessons, but he didn't care. He could already swim by then. In contrast, his parents were remorseful and kind. I remember they came around with a box of chocolates.' Her T-shirt flapped in the sea breeze. Awkwardly she withdrew her hand and smoothed her hair out of her eyes. 'My mother told me he collects the rubbish these days, so I think I outpaced him professionally, even if he is a better swimmer.'

He ran a finger down the side of her

face. The touch was almost unbearable and her heart was thundering. Colour shot into her face and she met his glance. Her heart pounded and she hoped his mother wasn't watching them. They were interrupted by the noisy arrival of Antonio and Alessa. Leandro dropped his hand and stood up. They'd come for a bucket for Gran. Leandro handed them one and nodded towards the nearby rock pools. 'You can get water there. No need to run back and forth to the sea.' They nodded enthusiastically and disappeared again.

He returned his attention to Emma. Emma looked at him and noticed the grains of dried sand on his brown arms. Emma longed to run her hands down his skin and brush them away. An invisible web of attraction was growing stronger between them. She tried to normalize the situation. 'I expect we all have a weakness of some kind, don't we?'

'Yes, I think you're right. And it doesn't always need to be a physical weakness, does it? I think my personal weakness is the Villa Bella Rosa. No matter how well it's doing, I worry. I know I'm doing the best I can, but it doesn't stop me continually worrying about the future.'

Emma hurried to reassure him. 'You've diversified your sources of income, and you're prepared to think about other ways of increasing profits. Some years will always be better than others; it's the same in any business.'

He nodded. 'Yes, I know. I hope one day to build up emergency funds, but I don't lose sleep over it like in the beginning. I realize that all farms face problems and complications all the time because we depend on nature, and no one can control that. Farming has always been hard and risky.'

She nodded. 'And despite that, you still decided to invest some money in restoring the paintings? Perhaps you should have hoarded that cash for emergencies.'

His smile was wide, his teeth

strikingly white in his tanned face, and her heart hammered foolishly. 'Perhaps.' He looked thoughtfully out to sea. 'I promised my father to take care of everything, and that means the house as well as the land. Your boss is a very persuasive man, and we can afford it at the moment.' He turned his attention to her face again. 'If I'd saved the money, we wouldn't have met, would we? That would've been a great pity. Are you trying to talk yourself out of a job by any chance?'

She laughed and hoped he was talking about himself when he used the expression 'we'. Her eyes twinkled when she replied. 'Heaven forbid! You're providing me with my bread and butter!'

'Talking of food, what about something to eat?' He studied her and then suddenly and quite unexpectedly, he leaned forward and kissed her softly. She loved the velvet warmth of his kiss and didn't want it to end.

She was aware of the tiny white lines at the corner of his eyes. She already knew she wanted to belong to this man and what he stood for — but it was impossible. They were worlds apart in several ways.

His brows arched mischievously as he gazed into her eyes, drew away and said softly, 'I promised not to do that again, didn't I? But there's something about you, Emma Lomax, that makes me forget myself.' He brushed the sand from his hands and looked out to sea. 'If you promise to forget about your fear of deep water, I'll stop worrying about the estate.'

'You know very well that neither of us can do that.'

They shared a smile and he got up. 'I'll fetch the others and tell them lunch is ready.'

Watching his easy strides as he drew away, Emma wished she could concentrate on something else other than Leandro when he was near, but it was impossible. His gentle kiss a moment ago had finally shattered her composure. Emma couldn't remember sharing her inner fears with someone so easily before. She usually avoided baring her soul to anyone, but it was so easy to talk to Leandro about anything and everything. She wondered why she didn't hesitate where he was concerned. Her thoughts lingered on his brief kiss and she tried to hold on to the memory because her body longed for more. Perhaps he was just playing with her emotions because she was available — but there was something else happening. Somehow she knew he felt comfortable with her and liked her. Was he aware of the effect he was having on her? He wasn't a womaniser; but then, didn't most men yield to temptation, given the chance and the opportunity?

She watched as he climbed the nearby rocks and gestured to the others. He looked like a Greek god. She busied herself with the plastic cups and food containers and tried to think rationally. Even if he was free, and even if he did like her a little, they had no time to get to know each other properly. Their lives were poles apart.

They shared a delicious lunch and the day seemed almost perfect. Emma moved to the shade of the rocks after lunch until the others persuaded her to play a game of crazy football with them. Leandro seemed to be having as much fun as Alessa and Antonio. Emma stirred uneasily as the thought that he'd make a great father flitted across her mind. The children wanted to go swimming again, so Leandro shrugged and obliged. His mother said she'd have a nap and promptly fell asleep.

Emma got up and met the other three with her finger to her lips when she saw them on their way back. Zarah was still asleep. They dried off quietly and Leandro signalled they could take a stroll along the beach. Emma nodded. It would keep the children busy and they could then make all the noise they wanted to again.

They walked as far as the next bend, the children racing ahead and gathering shells on the way. The sea was a clear blue and the cliffs jutted rudely out into the seawater. It felt comfortable to walk at his side. Shoulders touching, she was astounded by the thrill she felt just being with him. He told her about his father, and a little about the family's history.

'I'm impressed. Franca never ceases to inform me you are a descendent of a long line of Italian aristocrats.'

He laughed. 'The title Marchese de Luca doesn't count for much these days. It sounds impressive, but it doesn't put food on the table. I'm an estate manager.' He stopped to pick up a shell. 'By the way, I took your advice. I told Marco it was about time he got involved with the estate business and that he should take over some aspect of the work exclusively. He said he'd let me know what he'd like to do after he'd given it some thought.'

She looked up into his face and laughed. 'Did he? Hurrah! Wait and see. He'll surprise you one day, I'm sure.'

He dropped the shell into her palm.

'Will that do as payment for your advisory services?'

Emma closed her fist around it tightly and swallowed a lump in her throat. 'That will do nicely. Thank you!'

When they reached the point where the rocks cut off any further progress, the children waited. They scrambled up the mottled surface and began to search the pools and crevices. Emma climbed up after them, stopped to push some wind-whipped hair out of her face, and then proceeded to watch the waves dashing against the nearby speckled boulders. She was intensely aware of Leandro standing with his hands thrust into his pockets when he joined her. When they jumped down to turn back, he reached his hand to help her. He held his hands around her waist for longer than necessary. They stared at each other and the world stopped turning. Her heart thumped wildly out of control. They viewed each other silently for a second before the children brought them back to earth and he released her again.

'Can we have some ice-cream?'

Leandro groaned artificially. 'Okay! But only if Gran is awake and she agrees.'

When they got back, Zarah was already on the lookout for them. Leandro explained where they'd been and what the children wanted. She smiled. They collected the rugs and everything else and took them back to the car, before strolling down a promenade edged with flowering shrubs and dotted with cafés and restaurants. They chose one with outside tables overlooking the cliffs.

The children took ages to choose their gelato. Emma's turned out to be one of the best ice-creams she'd ever tasted, and Leandro was amused by the expressions of bliss on her face as her ice-cream quickly disappeared.

By the time they ambled back to the mini-van, the sun had lost its power. Looking at his watch, Leandro declared it was time to go. The children groaned and wanted to go back to the beach but he was firm. 'It's time to go!'

Once they were on the road, Alessa's head fell to the side and she slept. Antonio stared listlessly out of the window. The journey home was quieter, but Emma was grateful for the chance to think silently about Leandro and her feelings for him. When they drew up outside the door, Alessa woke up and yawned. The children said cheerio to Emma and disappeared into the house.

The sound of an approaching car ended the harmony. A bottle-green sports car squealed to a stop, and Mariella got out. She looked at Leandro reproachfully and pecked at his cheek. 'Why didn't you invite me? I would have loved to have come.'

'Because you always complain about everything whenever we go to the beach. Last time you came, you grumbled constantly about how demanding the children were and how the sand got into everything.'

She ran her fingers down his arm. 'They were smaller then. I think I can cope with them much better these days.'

Emma's happy mood took a decided downward turn. Mariella couldn't help it, but she often managed to ruin Emma's cheerful mood.

'Hello, Zarah. Emma.'

Emma nodded and tried to offer her a friendly smile. 'Hello.' She went to collect her bag from the boot of the car.

Mariella moved next to Leandro's mother. She waved a piece of paper in Leandro's direction. 'I've been busy while you've been out enjoying yourself. Look!'

'Have you? Doing what?'

'The label.'

'What label?'

'The label for the packets of sunflower seeds. We talked about it, remember?'

Emma felt anger building up inside. Her fingers tightened around her bag as she viewed them through the car window. Leandro took the paper and then nodded at Mariella. 'Not bad!'

Emma suddenly realized Leandro had told Mariella about her idea and Mariella had made use of the information to demonstrate how interested she was, and how she wanted to help him and the estate. Emma longed to snatch the paper out of his hands and complain, but she forced herself to rearrange things in the boot until her anger faded to a manageable level. She shouldered her bag and joined the others.

Leandro showed her the paper. 'What do you think?'

She'd already vocally suggested an idea to him one day, and even made a rough sketch. Looking at Mariella's efforts, she saw that Mariella had used her suggestion. The family's coat of arms was a faded shadow in the background, and some sunflowers were printed in bright colours in the foreground. She looked at it briefly and shoved it back petulantly into his hands.

His brows lifted when he noted her

reaction and he frowned.

She turned away without comment and said, 'Thank you, Zarah, for a very enjoyable day. I think the children had a great time, and so did I. I'll skip dinner this evening if you don't mind. I'm not very hungry after all the picnic food.'

Zarah smiled at her thoughtfully. 'I enjoyed it too, and I hope we'll do something similar again before you leave.'

Emma walked into the house saying 'Good night' to no one in particular.

Mariella's voice drifted over her shoulder. 'That means you have an empty chair at your table. Franca is making one of my favourite dishes this evening. May I join you instead of Emma? It will give us a chance to talk.'

Zarah said, 'Of course, Mariella. You are very welcome. Do you want to phone home and tell them?'

She tossed her hair. 'They know where I am.'

★   ★   ★

With her back like a ramrod and her eyes fixed ahead, Emma hurried up the stairs to her room. Once she closed the door, she leaned against it and felt tears at the back of her eyes. She stifled them. It had been a perfect day until a few minutes ago. Perhaps she was just being childish. She stared out of the window. Mariella could have suggested marketing the sunflowers long ago, but she'd never shown any interest in helping the estate. She knew that lots of people in Tuscany sold sunflower seeds in shops and at markets as a sideline. It was just another spiteful attempt to outshine Emma.

15

Next morning, after an unsettled night, Emma met Marco on his way out when she came down the stairs. 'Good lord, you're awake already — at this time in the morning!'

He grinned. 'I had another date with Ambra yesterday, and I keep thinking about her all the time. I can't sleep properly anymore.' He lifted his thumb and first finger to his lips. 'What a girl. I think I'm in love at last.'

Emma laughed. 'Tell me about it in six months' time.'

'No, I'm serious. Wait until you meet her. I'm going to surprise her now, and give her a lift to work.' Emma laughed as she watched him cheerfully heading for his car.

★   ★   ★

She found her usual solitary breakfast waiting for her in the inner courtyard. The weather was perfect. Franca came with her coffee. Fussing around with the tablecloth, she said, 'Mariella turned up after you left yesterday and she was mad that she hadn't been invited.'

Emma looked down at her cup and then at Franca. 'Yes, she mentioned she'd been looking for Leandro when we came back.'

'Mariella thinks she holds sway over him. She doesn't. He won't be steamrolled into anything.'

Emma looked at her watch and got up. 'Back to the grindstone!' Seeing Franca's puzzled expression, she explained, 'Back to work!'

She went to the shed and was determined to concentrate on work. When she stopped some time later, the morning air was still fresh and cool. She glanced outside the open doors across the landscape, still wrapped in the hazy veil of the morning mists.

She heard Leandro's footsteps nearing, and tensed. Normally she felt immediate delight, but her present mood was still clouded over. She didn't look up when he came in.

'My sister has just come to fetch the children.'

Emma gave him a brief glance and nodded. Trying not to sound uptight, she said, 'They weren't looking forward to going back to school, were they?'

He stuck his hands in his pockets. 'No.'

Emma went on working. She didn't want to talk; she would probably sound resentful.

'You're very quiet today. Something wrong?'

She shook her head. 'No, should it be?'

He shifted uneasily. 'I had the feeling you were upset because Mariella waved that label around yesterday. Does it matter who designed it?'

Despite everything, Emma was pleased that he'd sensed what was bothering her. She shrugged. 'Probably not, but as the original suggestion came from me, it was annoying to find Mariella was suddenly in charge and used exactly the same motif. I didn't realize you'd discussed it with her.'

He stiffened. 'I wasn't aware I had to inform you about who I talk to, and about what.'

She coloured. 'I didn't mean that and you know it. If I'd known you'd arranged for Mariella to do it, I wouldn't have bothered or been taken by surprise.'

'I didn't know she intended to do anything. Aren't you making a fuss about something that's insignificant?'

She turned and faced him. 'I am not making a fuss. You started to talk about it, not me. Mariella could have suggested the idea long ago, and organized it from beginning to end. She didn't. She just used my idea. Is it surprising that I felt annoyed?'

He exhaled noticeably and exclaimed, 'Why are women so complicated? I've known her all my life. She just wanted to help. I don't suppose she stopped to consider she was using your idea and locking you out of events.'

Emma turned away. 'Why don't we leave it at that, then. I don't want to quarrel with you about Mariella.'

He offered her a crumb of an apology. 'I didn't know what she was planning, Emma, until she turned up yesterday.'

She threw some cleaning pads into the bin and went to get a new supply. Over her shoulder, she said, 'Then perhaps you should tell Mariella to ask you first before she does anything similar again. By the way, women are not difficult. Some women are more difficult than others; there's a big difference.'

There was silence for a moment, and then she heard the door bang on his way out.

Emma slumped against a nearby storage bin and wished she'd been more compliant. He'd noticed her mood last night and tried to clear the air, but she'd now merely annoyed him. Straightening, she told herself it was right to object. If he prized Mariella's support more than hers, she could live with that; but she didn't intend to let Mariella trample over her feelings, and she wouldn't pretend she didn't care.

★　★　★

Next time they met, he was as polite as ever. He didn't mention the labels again, and neither did she. She wished she wasn't jealous whenever she saw Mariella heading towards the stables looking for him.

She followed the other women into the living room one evening after dinner. Zarah told her there was documentary about a safari park in Africa on TV and Franca wanted to see it too. Emma could enjoy a programme about wild animals without understanding Italian, so she agreed to join them. Leandro didn't; he went out to the stables.

During one of the breaks, Zarah said,

'I'm going to Siena tomorrow and Franca is coming with me. Why don't you take a break from your work and come with us?'

Emma liked the idea. It would be good to get away, and to see Siena before she left.

Zarah continued, 'We don't go very often, but sometimes we stock up on things that we can't find in the local shops — special oils, sausages and such. We enjoy the bustle, but by day's end we know exactly why we like living here and not there.'

Emma said, 'I'd like to come. Thanks for asking me.'

'If you want to shop, join us; but if you want to look around the town, we can leave you near the main square and meet you there later. Siena is a tourist's Mecca.'

Emma nodded. 'I can go shopping anytime at home. I'd prefer to explore the town.'

Next morning it was fine and cool when they set out. Emma offered to drive, but Zarah de Luca brushed her offer aside. 'I'm used to the traffic and know where to park. Another time, perhaps?' Emma didn't think there'd be another time, but she nodded.

It was a pleasant journey and Emma viewed the passing scenery with interest. They exited from the highway and followed some parking signs to a huge parking garage called Il Campo. To her surprise, there was plenty of room. It was only a five-minute walk to the centre, and they agree to meet up again for the return journey at the same spot later that afternoon. With a cheerful smile, they left her and went on their way.

Emma bought a city guide at a souvenir shop and began to explore. She headed towards the large fan-shaped Piazza del Campo and was surprised by its sheer size. Siena was certainly one of the prettiest medieval towns Emma had ever seen.

There were exclusive boutiques and expensive antique shops in the side streets leading off the main square, and Emma enjoyed looking around. In one of the windows, she saw an enticing polished leather handbag that shone like rusty gold. The shop owner soon realized he had a customer on the hook. In the end, after employing his special brand of Italian charm, she finally capitulated and gave him her credit card. He packed it into a soft cloth bag and then into a paper carrier bag.

Strolling back towards the Piazza del Campo, Emma was startled when she heard her name. She looked around and saw it was Mariella. Emma masked her exasperation. She'd been enjoying the freedom and the atmosphere. She didn't want Mariella to spoil her day. 'Oh hello, Mariella.'

Mariella was wearing a figure-hugging dress. Her make-up was more pronounced than usual and her jet-black hair was pinned into a perfect chignon. She looked like a model from a glossy magazine. Emma smoothed her own linen trousers and shaped jacket and was glad that, for once, she felt stylish. It was the only smart outfit she'd brought with her.

'What are you doing here?' Mariella looked at Emma's plastic bag. 'Been shopping?'

'No, not really.' She held the plastic bag aloft. 'Only this. It was a spur-of-the-moment buy. I came with Leandro's mother and Franca. They're shopping, and we'll meet up later when it's time to go home. I'm merely viewing the attractions.'

Mariella nodded in the direction of the nearby boutiques with their exclusive window displays. 'It's a very expensive part of town here, but you can find some wonderful things if you know where to look, and search long enough.'

'Visiting expensive boutiques has never been one of my pastimes.'

Mariella ran a knowledgeable eye over Emma's clothes. 'Yes, I can tell that. Your outfit is nice but it's very simple, isn't it?'

Her remark was rude. Emma couldn't

decide if that was the intention or not, but she decided not to waste time quarrelling and bickering. The two of them simply weren't on the same wavelength. 'I don't think clothes are that important. I've never earned enough to afford designer clothes, and even if I did, I'd be reluctant to spend a lot of money on haute couture unless it was very classical and I could wear it for years and years. You can buy nice things without bankrupting yourself.'

Mariella's voice tinkled. 'Perhaps, but Italian men like Leandro expect their women to look first-class. Second-best or second-class won't do.'

Emma shrugged. 'Does he? Do they? Are you sure? I presume Italian men are no different to any other men. They don't choose their girlfriends because of their dress sense. Some men I know have girlfriends, or fiancées, with eccentric dress tastes, but the men still love them for who they are.'

Looking irritated, Mariella's eyebrows lifted. 'You seem to think you know all about Italian men. How long have you been here? Three weeks, four weeks? How many Italian men do you know?'

'Not many, but I do know that men usually end up with someone who matches their lifestyle. If he's a bank manager, his wife will have a wardrobe for dinner parties and social gatherings. If she's married to a farmer, she'll have more practical clothes. She'll need to work alongside her husband. I know, because my father is a farmer. My mum helps him dressed in jeans if she's needed, but she still dolls up for special occasions.'

From her expression, Emma could tell Mariella didn't agree. Her stuck-up attitude maddened Emma. She couldn't help herself asking, 'By the way, what do you do?'

Mariella stiffened. 'Do? What do you mean?'

'What's your job? How do you earn your living?'

Moving her exclusive bag nervously,

she said agitatedly, 'I help my father with the office work.'

'And that keeps you busy? Signora de Luca only needs a couple of days in a month to organize the villa's paperwork and she does it on her own. Is your father's estate bigger or smaller?'

Without replying, Mariella studied the tips of her high-heeled shoes and then her gold watch. 'I must rush. I'm meeting an old school-friend. I want to be back in time to go out riding with Leandro later on. You don't ride, do you? Pity about that! . . . Enjoy yourself.'

Emma replied automatically, 'Thanks.' She knew that Mariella didn't care if she enjoyed herself or not, but Emma was glad to see her go. She glanced at the guide and headed towards the Duomo, the local cathedral. The crypt contained some beautiful frescos. Studying them in the cooler temperatures of the vault distracted her for quite a while and helped keep her mind off other things.

Afterwards, she returned to the Piazza del Campo and sat down at an open-air café. The information in her city guide was spot-on — the ground did slope. She looked up at the startling blue sky above the russet tones of the buildings and ordered a pricey gelato and mineral water. It was hot and the ice cubes in the glass tinkled as she drained it almost in one gulp. The lemon-flavoured gelato was heavenly. She studied the local souvenir shops catering to the never-ending stream of tourists from all over the world with their Tuscan pottery and bright post-cards. She felt completely stress-free.

Reflecting on her meeting with Mariella, she mused that Leandro deserved someone better. Mariella wouldn't change her costly lifestyle, and if he continued to manage the estate's income as carefully as he was doing, they'd probably fight constantly. They'd grown up together, so he couldn't pretend he didn't know what she was like.

She jumped when the object of her thoughts catapulted her out of her musings with his familiar deep voice.

16

'What are you doing here?'

Seeing him so suddenly turned her knees to jelly. She was surprised that she managed to answer sensibly, 'I'm playing tourist. I came with your mother and Franca. They wanted to do some shopping and I decided to play truant for a day.' She looked around the square. 'Siena is very impressive. I love it.'

'With your artistic background, you probably enjoy it more than most people.'

All of a sudden, her surroundings seemed even more vibrant and she felt excited inside. The effect he had on her was astounding. 'And why are you here? Are you skiving too?' She tossed her annoyance about the label overboard, and waited. He laughed, and she knew why she liked him so much. He was damned attractive, intelligent, level-headed, and a very nice person to boot, once you got to know him. He was straightforward, and nothing like the kind of emotional Italian everyone saw in Italian films. Marco came closer to that description.

He looked down at her gelato. 'Since you just admitted you're dodging your work, you can hardly accuse me of neglecting mine. That's the pot calling the kettle black, as you say in English.' He sat down in the neighbouring chair. 'I have time for a coffee.'

Emma was delighted that the atmosphere between them was so relaxed and friendly again. She asked, 'Do you have a legitimate reason to be here?' Emma wondered fleetingly if it might be Mariella.

She was relieved when he said, 'I came to meet someone, to arrange to borrow a harvesting machine for the sunflowers.'

'Oh, I see.'

He gestured to a waiter and ordered his coffee. Emma looked at his compelling dark eyes, firm features and confident set of his shoulders. He had an aura of purpose and quiet assurance about him that she loved. When his coffee came, she thanked fate silently for bringing him this way at exactly this moment. She simply enjoyed his company more than that of anybody she'd ever known.

He put his arm along the back of her chair and he told her more about Siena, and the famous horse races that took place in this square in July and August. It was obvious why the event held a special appeal for him.

He twisted a strand of her hair around his finger and her heart hammered foolishly. His touch alone sent a shiver down her spine. 'Your hair is extremely attractive, like molten gold. I never thought to ask you if you can ride.' She shook her head. 'Would you like to try?'

'I've never thought about it. I do know that keeping a horse is an expensive activity. I have a friend who seems to spend most of her income on feeding and stabling her horse, and paying vet's fees.'

A passing Italian gave her a wink. Leandro noticed and gave the other man a warning look. He leaned back and stuck his long legs out in a straight line. 'It's my weakness. One I'd be reluctant to give up unless we're on the brink of bankruptcy. If you were here long enough, I'd teach you to ride.' He studied her face carefully. His breath fanned her face.

His closeness was a drug, lulling her into euphoria. She met his glance. 'Then it's just as well that I'm not. I'd be a rotten pupil.'

'I don't think so.' He looked at his watch. 'I've got to meet someone in ten minutes on the other side of the town. See you back at the villa.' He got up and dropped an unexpected kiss on her forehead.

She was infinitely relieved that they were friends again. She cleared her throat while pretending her emotions were completely under control. 'Hey!

What about your coffee? Who's paying?'

He grinned. 'You are!'

He was already on the move. She grumbled loud enough for him to hear, 'The sheer cheek of the man!'

★   ★   ★

When she met up with the older women later, she mentioned she'd met Mariella and Leandro; but the women were tired, loaded with bags of shopping, and not inclined to ask many questions. Emma lightened their load and they walked back to the car. An hour later, they reached the Villa Bella Rosa again. Apart from meeting Mariella, Emma had enjoyed the whole day. She loved Siena and she'd had the bonus of being alone with Leandro for a few minutes.

After a shower, she checked the painting before they had their 'makeshift' evening meal of various local cheeses, olives and sausages, along with the villa's own Chianti and crispy bread. Marco was out on another date with Ambra, and Leandro wasn't around to share their evening meal either. She remembered Mariella had suggested they go out riding together that evening. She didn't like the idea at all.

Emma could tell the other women were tired after their excursion. She left promptly after the meal and settled down with a paperback.

★   ★   ★

Next morning she was busy with her work when she heard the clatter of horse hoofs. For a moment she was optimistic and hoped it was Leandro, but the feeling of exhilaration faded when Mariella strode in. Her white silk blouse rippled across her firm breasts and she slapped her whip against her tight-fitting trousers. 'I'm looking for Leandro. Have you seen him?'

Emma, dressed in scruffy jeans and a messy T-shirt, looked up. 'No, I haven't. Ask Franca. She usually knows what he's doing and where he is.' She turned back to mixing another batch of solvent.

Mariella didn't leave. She stayed and uttered, 'It won't do you any good.'

Emma looked up in surprise. 'I beg your pardon?'

'Chasing Leandro. It won't do any good.' Mariella shrugged. 'You might trap him into a quick affair, but you'll be gone again soon. It wouldn't be worth it.'

The air seemed to leave Emma's lungs and she must have looked like a fish out of water. She was rendered completely speechless for a moment because it was so unexpected. She stared at her in astonishment. Mariella continued to throw looks as sharp as knives at her.

Eventually, Emma managed to say, 'I'm sorry, Mariella, but I don't know what you mean, or what you're talking about.'

Mariella moved to lean against the old side table with the wilted sunflowers. The vase wobbled for a moment before it righted itself again. 'He has to concentrate on the estate. He doesn't need a tête-à-tête with a romantically dazed Englishwoman.'

Emma stared at her and decided she was sorry for anyone who married this woman. She was spiteful, possessive, and vindictive. She'd give him no room to breathe or to live his own kind of life.

Mariella's voice droned on. 'Leandro has had brief affairs in the past, but don't build up any hopes; not unless you're satisfied with a quick trip between the sheets and empty arms afterwards.'

Emma's temper grew. You didn't talk about someone you loved like that. She made him sound like a gigolo and he wasn't. Straightening, Emma said, 'I'm not hoping for any kind of special relationship. He's my employer. He's polite and kind. I like him, but I'm certainly not looking for more, and I'm sure he isn't either. Why are you talking to me like this?'

Mariella faced her with a bland expression and unreadable eyes. 'Because I thought I should warn you. I don't want you to get hurt.'

Emma didn't believe her. Mariella's claws were out. She was in love with him herself, or trying to isolate him from any other woman who got too close. He was her best chance of a meal ticket to a comfortable marriage with financial security. He needed someone to share the load, not someone who would try to restrict him. Mariella under-estimated Leandro's intelligence and his determination. If he'd had affairs in the past, Emma was sure he'd liked the woman in question at the time. Emma didn't believe it had been merely a tête-à-tête devoid of any emotion, just to get someone into bed. According to Franca, Mariella had dumped him to find someone with a higher income bracket when things were difficult. Emma hoped he wouldn't forget that and marry someone who loved him for who he was, not what he represented.

Emma was certain that she loved him, but she was a temporary English employee who didn't even speak his language. She wasn't stupid enough to ignore reality. She needed to listen to her brain and not her heart. She didn't need Mariella's biting remarks to remind her there was no future for her here. She didn't want to listen to any more either. She turned demonstratively away from Mariella and ignored her. She picked up a scalpel and went on with her work. Silence settled between them. After a moment or two, she heard Mariella closing the door behind her with unnecessary force.

Emma carried on with the other woman's words spinning around in her brain. On reflection, she only hoped her own feelings weren't transparent. It'd be embarrassing if others noticed that she was hooked on Leandro.

★   ★   ★

When the sun grew stronger, she put the tops on her bottles and went towards the main house. It was silent, and she sidled down the corridor to the kitchen. Franca looked up when she came in. Enzo had just brought in some vegetables for the evening meal and he gave Emma a toothy smile before he said something to his wife in Italian and left.

Franca said, 'There's fresh orange juice in the fridge.'

'Sounds wonderful!' Emma helped herself. 'Where are all the others?'

'Zarah is visiting a friend. Leandro has taken Marco to introduce him to some people who run the local co-operative for olive production.' She tilted her head and smiled. 'Marco is showing a bit of interest at last, and Leandro is encouraging him. Marco wants to take over the olive production. That will take some of the pressure off Leandro, and it's about time too.'

Emma took a cold sip and nodded. 'That's good. Perhaps it's what Marco needs too — a bit more responsibility.' Franca listened while kneading pastry. Emma was still seething about Mariella's visit. 'Mariella just called. She wanted to know where Leandro was, and in passing she told me not to get the wrong idea about him.'

Franca's hands paused in mid-air. 'She did what?'

'She said she wanted to warn me so that I wouldn't get hurt. She suggested Leandro would pick me up, have a quick affair and then drop me like a hot potato.'

Franca looked pensive and then chuckled. 'She's getting nervous. Don't worry about what she says. She wouldn't act so stupidly if she had more confidence and she knew that things were going her way. I always said the boy had too much sense to get caught in her net.'

'Leandro and I get on well, but I'll be gone in a couple of weeks. I know that, he knows it, and so does she. I don't know why she made a fool of herself like that.'

'I do.'

Emma smiled. 'I take that as a compliment.' She washed out the glass and left it on the draining board. 'I'm going to have a shower and a rest until it gets cooler.'

Franca nodded and continued to knead the pastry and mull over the new information.

* * *

Later that afternoon Emma returned to the shed. The temperature was not absolutely ideal for cleaning pictures, but she had to do the best she could. It would have been better to handle them in a cool dust-free environment, but she tried to minimize the dust and choose the coolest part of every day.

She'd been busy for a while and completed a few more inches of the painting. Leandro's steps interrupted her concentration and she looked up and smiled. Her smile faded a little when she noticed his expression.

17

'Hi! Is something wrong?'

'You tell me! Franca has just repeated some mad story you told her about Mariella warning you not to get involved with me.' His brows were in a straight line and the skin was taut across his cheekbones.

Her mouth was dry and she swallowed hard. 'I wish Franca hadn't passed that on. I didn't want her to. It wasn't a story. Mariella did warn me to back off and leave you alone.' She coloured. 'She was here this morning. She was looking for you.'

'I can't believe Mariella would discuss me in that way with anyone. I've known her all her life. She knows we have an understanding to respect each other, and not to carry tales.'

Emma shrugged. 'If you don't believe it, then just forget it. If you ask her, she'll probably deny it anyway. I don't know why she said anything in the first place. She pretended it was for my own good, and I didn't believe that either.' Facing him squarely, she insisted, 'Whether you believe it or not, it did happen!'

A muscle jerked in his face. 'It's extremely difficult to believe.'

The colour shot into her face. 'In other words, you think I made it up? That I'm lying? Why should I? I don't lie — but if you think I do, ignore what I told Franca and carry on.' From his expression, she decided she didn't want to argue with him anymore. She held his gaze.

He took an abrupt step towards her and his nearness made her heart jump in her chest. He reached up and unexpectedly cradled her face for a second before their lips met. The kiss sent shock waves through her body. She stared up at him and leaned against the tautness of his body. She had a burning desire, an aching need, for him. His uneven breath was warm on her face.

He dropped his arms and stepped back. He stated, 'There's some kind of chemical reaction between us that I can't explain and I can't control.' His expression was dark and he viewed her silently. She waited, hoping for more of him. She waited for a peaceful discussion. She waited for whatever he was willing to give.

He ran a hand down his face and looked slightly confused. Turning swiftly, he went through the door, leaving her to wonder if it had really happened. She ran her fingers across her lips and her heart beat too fast with love for this complex man. It was clear that his head governed his heart. He liked to have everything under control.

She leaned on the table and her thoughts alternated between hopelessness and euphoria. Her cheeks were hot and her pulse was still too fast. She tried to concentrate on her work.

★ ★ ★

The evening meal was quieter than usual. Leandro and Emma didn't say much to each other. No one noticed because Marco and his mother were busy with other things. His mother chatted about the neighbour she'd visited that afternoon, and Marco told them about his latest girlfriend, Ambra, and her family. They owned a small farm not far away. Ambra's brother and father farmed it together.

Emma went to her room, pleading a headache. She hated a situation where Leandro and she avoided each other wherever they could. Mariella's attempt to separate them was working. He wanted to believe Mariella, and he didn't want to believe her. His belief in Mariella was stronger than their friendship. If the situation remained that way, the rest of her stay wouldn't be easy, but somehow she would get through it.

*   *   *

For a couple of days Emma and Leandro both kept a polite distance and neither of them mentioned Mariella again.

Marco brought Ambra to lunch on Sunday. She was a very pretty girl with short black curly hair, deep blue eyes and a rosebud mouth. Emma could understand why Marco was smitten. She wasn't just pretty; she was clever too. Her English was excellent and she worked in the offices of a well-known local lawyer.

After they left, Franca commented that she thought Ambra wasn't the usual flippant type of female Marco brought home. The way that Marco's eyes never left Ambra's face made Emma wonder if he'd met his match at last.

* * *

With the progress of summer, activity around the estate increased. The women were busy bottling fruit, preserving vegetables and making jam. Mushrooms in oil, beans, garlic, tomatoes in all shapes and forms, courgettes, aubergines — the list was never-ending. One of everyone's favourite preserves was tomato jam. Franca used a recipe handed down from her grandmother, and it was delicious. Every time Emma went into the kitchen, something else was on the production line.

She went to Florence on Sunday. She arrived early in the morning in the hope of avoiding hordes of other tourists. She parked on the hill opposite, as Marco had suggested, and then walked down-hill, across the Ponte Vecchio, and into the city.

To her disappointment, Florence was already packed. There were long queues waiting to get into the Uffizi Gallery. Emma decided the real statue of David would have to wait for another day. She photographed the copy of it outside the Palazzo Vecchio. She was content to wander around, view the squares and medieval streets on her own, and marvel at everything. By mid-afternoon she was so tired that she made her way back to the jeep. She vowed to come back one day. She compared her more peaceful visit to Siena, and how she'd met Leandro there. Everything good she'd experienced seemed to have to do with Leandro.

*   *   *

The second painting was already looking in first-class shape. She'd cleaned it and was now restoring tiny flakes of matching paint. An illuminated magnifying glass was her most valuable tool.

She kept in touch with Maurice and supplied him with constant photos and progress reports. He seemed satisfied with whatever she told him and he was always ready with additional tips or advice if she asked him. The weather in the UK wasn't so good. Maurice envied her the warmth and the sun. He was looking forward tremendously to having his plaster cast removed. He told her, 'It itches like hell, and I can't go on scratching it with Betty's knitting needle much longer. I'll go barmy if I don't get rid of it soon!'

She hadn't seen much of Mariella since the day she'd come with her warning. Emma hadn't missed her. Emma saw Leandro every day, but ever since Mariella's remarks, he was more formal and slightly distant. He was never unfriendly, just cooler in his attitude.

He was also very busy, as all the other farmers in Tuscany were as the summer progressed. They checked weather reports every day, discussed prices, organized buyers, hired machinery and tended the various crops constantly. The fields of sunflowers were now a sea of gold. Emma's sunflowers in the pottery vase had died away, but she saved some of their seeds to plant next year in some pots at home.

The olive harvest was in November or December, so she'd miss that entirely. She'd most likely miss the wine harvest and probably the sunflower harvest in September too. It all depended on how fast she could finish the third painting once she started on it.

One afternoon, while checking her emails, she saw one from her mother, and another from an unknown addressee. She sent her mother a few lines and a couple of photos and then turned her attention to the unknown email address. It had the suffix 'it', so it came from someone in Italy. She hesitated but then opened it. To her delight, she found it was from Alessa.

'Dear Emma, I hope you're well. We are, and looking forward to the holidays. I'm hoping you can help me. I've lost a silver necklace. I remember wearing it when we visited Gran last time, but I can't find it. Could you check to see if I dropped it in the old house? If I lost it in the fields we'll never find it, but it could be in the house. I can't ask Gran to look — she gave it to me, and I don't want her to know unless I'm certain it's gone. Perhaps you'll check the

cottage for me? Thank you very much. Your friend, Alessa.'

Emma smiled and decided to take a look for her that very same evening, after dinner. She often went for a walk at the end of the day. She'd never gone back to the cottage but she knew how to get there now, and she had plenty of time to get there and back before it got dark.

Dinner was a light-hearted affair because Marco had finally decided to take over the Villa Bella Rosa's olive production. He was full of harvesting plans, planting new trees and modernizing the oil-press, as soon as finances allowed. Leandro looked pleased and toasted him. Emma liked Marco and she liked his light-hearted attitude to life. He was a contrast to Leandro, but he was growing up fast and it looked like he was ready to take responsibility. She lifted her glass and smiled across the table at Zarah de Luca, who looked proudly at her two sons.

She met Franca in the corridor as she was about to set out for the house, and told her where she was going and why. 'Don't tell anyone, especially not Zarah. Alessa doesn't want her to know she might have lost the necklace. Perhaps I'll find it for her.'

Franca nodded. 'You know where to find the key?'

'Yes.'

18

Emma set off and enjoyed her quiet walk through the fields. It was still warm and the breezes carried the smell of the land and its products. Tuscany had found its way into her heart. She was already determined to come back. She'd look for somewhere to stay near Siena. Perhaps she'd be able to afford a couple of weeks next year.

Emma reached the crest of the hill and looked down at the lonely cottage as it waited silently in the first shadows of the day. There was a feeling of isolation and abandonment about it today. She looked up at the sky briefly. It wouldn't be long before the setting sun painted the heavens aflame, and then the building would be alone in the darkness again. She wondered who'd lived there long ago. They must have led a very austere existence.

She skipped down the slope and reached her destination. She found the key and inserted it into the lock. It was hard to turn because the lock was rusty and needed some oil, but she finally managed, lifted the latch and went inside. She had a torch but didn't need it. There was still enough light when she opened the inside shutters and folded them against the walls. She looked outside briefly through the bars as she did so. Starting to search the rooms for the necklace, she found no trace of it downstairs. Upstairs, perhaps?

Emma climbed the narrow stairs to the small anteroom with doors leading off to the right and the left. She checked the first, and was startled when she heard the door slam downstairs. It wasn't windy.

With her heart in her mouth, she dashed back down the stairs. The two rooms were empty. As she went towards the door, something crashed through the window-pane onto the flagstones in the centre of the room and burst into flames. A smell of burning petrol filled the air and the smoke from its fire was thick and acrid. Emma began to cough. The fierce flames reached hungrily towards the brittle beams and sent hot sparks in all directions. Emma instinctively began to stamp out the flames, and struggled to remove her cotton jacket at the same time. She used it to beat the flames and a few minutes later she was relieved to see she'd been successful.

Finally, she managed to suffocate the last remaining glimmers. Her jacket was burnt and ruined, but the fire from the bottle was now a heap of smoking remains. She kicked the residue apart, and bits of glass and the charred remains flew across the flagstones. Leaving things, she rushed to the door to lift the latch and found it was no use; the door was locked. She tried several times before she shivered and began to comprehend that someone had deliberately locked her in. Someone wanted to set fire to the cottage when she was inside.

With growing panic, she ran to one of the windows. She couldn't see anyone, but straining against the bars to see some of the surrounding countryside, she heard the sound of hoof beats, far off on the crest of one of the nearby hills.

It would soon be dark. She went from one room to the next, trying to budge the safety bars. They were tightly bolted, even if they looked rusted. There wasn't enough space for her to squeeze between the bars, and she could tell it was futile to even try. She closed the inner shutters again in case the culprit returned and tried to throw another missile inside. The closed shutters made everything more gloomy and sinister.

She tried the door again. She peered through the keyhole and saw the key wasn't in place. If it had been, she could have prodded it out and found something to shove under the door to catch it. There was no point in shouting. The cottage was too far from the villa or any other building, and also hidden from sight. No one came this way regularly unless they were checking the olive trees nearby or working in the fields. There was no water and nothing to eat. Perhaps no one would find her before it was too late.

For a moment she was scared stiff; but then, despite the feeling of panic, she remembered Franca. She'd told Franca she was coming here. Franca would be her guardian angel. When she didn't come for breakfast, or Franca didn't find her in the workshop, she'd remember Emma told her she was going to the cottage the night before.

Feeling slightly better, a few tears of frustration escaped and ran down her face. She rubbed them away. Her legs were bright pink and stinging in places. She looked around desperately for something to prise the door open with, or for a tool to dislodge one of the safety bars so she could climb out through the window. There was nothing apart from some bits of rotten furniture.

Resigning herself to a long wait, she went back upstairs. The smell of burning wasn't as strong up here and she had a better view out of the windows. The tiny dormer windows were built into the stonework with criss-cross solid window frames, so there was no chance of escape here either. The stars were beginning to twinkle as the sky changed and nightfall descended. After a while, she sat down with her back against one of the walls. It wasn't comfortable, but the only other alternative was to stretch out on the floor. She was grateful that the moon sent its light to dispel the complete darkness. It wasn't really cold but she wrapped her arms around her body. At first, she was scared the wrongdoer would return. It kept her alert, and now and then she checked the part of the countryside she could see from the window.

Eventually tiredness took over. She slept fitfully for short periods, always waking in fear. She stood up and walked around in circles sometimes. The night seemed never-ending, and she welcomed the first streaks of dawn. Emma felt a little better when she imagined how Franca would miss her at breakfast time and probably check the workshop and her room.

Emma's legs stung from the burns. She had a lot of time to think and came to one conclusion: Mariella was behind it. Who else had ever shown her any animosity? Who else had she seen out riding locally, apart from Leandro? If it had been mischievous teenagers looking for somewhere to set on fire, they wouldn't pick a deserted cottage far away from the roads. They'd want people to see what was happening.

No one else had been hostile toward her. Mariella must have sent the bogus email and lured her into the trap. She couldn't prove it was Mariella, of course. The horse and its rider were too far off. If she aired her suspicions, how many people would believe her?

She held onto the bars downstairs

when she opened the shutters and felt the freshness of an early-morning breeze. She was thirsty and she was forced to go to the toilet in the corner of one of the downstairs rooms. The puddle made a dark stain on the flagging, but who'd notice?

The hours ticked by and she was euphoric when she saw Enzo hurrying down the slope of the hill. She waved out of the window and called his name, long before he actually reached the cottage. She heard him fumbling outside and then the key turned in the lock and she almost fell into his arms in relief. He wasn't very tall and she was on a level with his eyes. He proceeded to bombard her with a torrent of Italian and a couple of English phrases.

Looking at her dishevelled state and noticing the bright pink skin on her legs, he said, 'You are all right? What are doing here? Why are you locked inside this place? Franca sent me.'

Emma grabbed his arm, pulled him inside and pointed to the charred remnants of the fire. Astonishment and alarm were written all over his face. '*Dio!*' He pointed towards the Villa Bella Rosa. 'We go?'

She nodded and Enzo locked the door. He pocketed the key. The downstairs shutters were still closed. Enzo looked down and pointed at inflamed patches on her legs and back to the cottage. 'From fire?' Emma just nodded.

When they reached the villa, they went straight to the kitchen. Franca looked relieved when she saw them. She covered her mouth in shock when Enzo recounted what he'd seen. Franca manoeuvred Emma into a chair. '*Mio Dio!* Are you all right?'

Emma gave her a weak smile. 'I'm fine. My legs hurt but everything is all right now I'm here again.'

'Did you see who did it?'

Emma shrugged. She'd decided not to accuse Mariella. She had no proof.

Franca eyed her and then began to bustle around. She made Emma milk coffee that tasted like nectar, and Emma asked for more. She ate a sandwich, but wasn't really hungry. She was so glad to be back in Franca's kitchen. Franca continued to fuss around and offer her other food. Enzo disappeared and returned promptly with Zarah.

Zarah viewed Emma with a shocked expression. 'Good heavens, Emma! Enzo just told me what happened. You must have been frightened to death.'

'Yes, I was scared, but I'm okay again now.' She felt like crying but she held her tears in check.

'Who could do such a thing? It's unbelievable. It's terrible to think something like that happened on our estate.' She looked at Emma more carefully and examined the burns. 'They look painful, but I have a very good cream that will help. If you're still in pain later on, we'll go to the doctor's. Once you've had something to eat and drink, have a shower and lie down. Try to sleep for a while. Both of the men are out in the fields. I'll send for them; they ought to know. Perhaps we should call the police?

Emma smiled unsteadily. 'No, don't do that. There's no point in involving the police. I'm sure whoever did it left no clues. If you call the police, Leandro and Marco will only waste time having to deal with them. My legs are okay. They don't sting half as much as they did when it happened. Honestly, I'm fine, don't worry about me.'

Shaking her head sceptically, Zarah de Luca watched as Emma went upstairs.

Emma went straight to the bathroom. When she looked in the mirror, her face and arms were streaked with dirt, and she could smell the acrid smoke on her clothes and her hair. She didn't recognize herself. She scrubbed her skin under the shower and washed her hair. Feeling better and back in her room, she found a tube of cream on the bedside table and rubbed some of it carefully on her legs. She slipped beneath the cool sheets and in no time at all, she was fast asleep.

When she woke, it was early afternoon. Emma was uneasy for a second, but she recalled everything was all right and she was in safety again. Zarah's cream had helped. The tight, tingling feeling had almost disappeared.

She tidied up and went down to the kitchen with her bundle of smoke-filled clothes. When she popped her head around the door, Franca smiled, took the garments and said, 'I'll sort them out for you. How do you feel now?'

'Much better, thanks. Can I have some orange juice? I'm going to check how things are in the shed.'

Franca indicated to a jug on a side table. 'Help yourself. Wouldn't it be better to forget about work for today?'

Emma shook her head. 'I'd rather do something. It helps.'

Franca nodded. 'I understand. Come back if you need anything. Leandro went out to the cottage, but he couldn't find anything suspicious and no evidence of who did it.'

Emma shoved her hair out of her

face. 'I didn't think anyone would. I don't suppose anyone will ever know who it was.' She left Franca and went to her own work.

★   ★   ★

She studied the second picture. It was a delightful pastoral scene and now that more colours had been revealed again, it was a pleasure to look at.

Marco knocked on the doorframe and came in. 'Hi there! Are you all right, *bella*? It's unbelievable. Whoever did it must be a nutcase. If I find out who it was, I'll soon sort them out for you! I've never heard of anything similar ever happening around here before.'

She smiled. 'Thanks, Marco. I'm fine again, but I can't pretend that I'll go wandering far from the house on my own like that again.'

He nodded understandingly. 'If it was hooligans they won't come back. They'd be too afraid of getting caught.

It is better that you don't take any more chances, until we find out who it was.'

She smiled. 'I'll stay near the house in future. Are you off somewhere?'

'To see Ambra. I'm going to meet her at her office and take her for a surprise meal.'

'I like her. She's a nice, intelligent girl. Don't keep her waiting!'

'I agree. She's perfect. I think she's the one for me.'

Emma laughed. 'Then you definitely shouldn't keep her waiting. Get along with you!'

19

Emma worked for a while in silence and tried not to think about the cottage. His footsteps put an end to her reflections. When Leandro came in, he just regarded her carefully for a moment. He stepped closer then and took her chin in his hands. He dropped them after considering her eyes and her expression, and continued watching. Emma could only think how his touch left her with a desire for much more.

'How are you feeling? Thank heavens you told Franca where you were going. I imagine no one would have thought about checking the cottage for quite a while, and it could have been too late by then.'

She gave a shaky smile. 'I know. I thought about that myself. I'm okay now. I was frightened at first, but after I remembered I'd told Franca, I thought she would miss me and send someone to look for me.'

'Why did you go there in the first place?'

Emma explained.

'How does Alessa know your email address?'

She shrugged. 'I don't know. I didn't give it a second thought at the time. Children pick up things so fast these days. I assumed she'd just noticed it somewhere, or even found it on the company's website. I noticed the email had an 'it' suffix, and although I was surprised I just presumed it was genuine. It could have been from a potential customer about a new job. It could have been someone who had my address from Maurice. I didn't imagine for a moment there was any danger involved.'

'Is it still on your computer? Can you show me?'

She opened her computer and he read the email. Deep in thought, he muttered, 'It's a hell of a mystery.

Who'd do such a thing? And why? It must be from someone who knows you. Someone who knows you are here. Someone who planned it all very carefully.'

Emma concentrated on the drooping sunflowers and closed the computer again. She ignored his questioning expression and didn't comment. It didn't take long.

He asked, 'Are you hiding something? Do you think you know who it was?'

Emma hesitated. She wanted to avoid conflict, but he seemed to be able to read her expression. She had a feeling he wouldn't let it go until she told him what she believed. 'To be honest, I think it might have been Mariella.' His brows lifted and she became increasingly uncomfortable under his scrutiny. 'I heard a horse galloping away minutes after the fire broke out downstairs. She's the only other person apart from you who rides around the estate regularly. If I'd gone back upstairs straight away I might have had a better look, but I was too busy putting out the flames; and later whoever it was, was too far away for me to see.'

He ran his hand down his face. 'So you're just guessing? Are you sure this isn't just another round of 'Emma versus Mariella'?'

She didn't like his reaction. Her face flamed and she reminded herself that she was the victim and she was entitled to say what she thought. He'd asked if she suspected anyone. Did he think she was making it all up? Emma swallowed hard and said quickly, 'I have no proof, and I don't know why she'd want to do such a thing, but I do think it was her.'

'You have to admit that your subconscious could be playing a role in all this. You don't like her.'

Heatedly she said, 'And what if I don't? That's got nothing to do with it. I stayed friendly, even if it was sometimes an effort. Why should I want to target Mariella with something so serious? Once my work is finished, no one here will ever see me again. What good would it do me?'

His brows were a dark straight line. 'I don't know, but you have to give anyone the benefit of the doubt until there is proof. Perhaps you didn't hear hoof beats. Old tractors sometimes have a hollow beat. Perhaps it was one of those in nearby fields.'

Feeling her anger increasing by the minute and with bright red cheeks, she said, 'I have no hearing problems and I know exactly what I heard. It wasn't a tractor. Don't brush my words aside as if it was an impossibility. Perhaps you're just blinded because you've known her all your life, but I've seen how cruel and mean she can be. I don't care what you think — it is quite possible that it was Mariella.'

He said stiffly, 'Somehow I can't believe it.'

Snapping, she retorted, 'Then don't!' Nearing the truth, she continued, 'Maybe she feels jealous of me being here and misjudges the situation. Or do you think I locked myself in the cottage and tried to send it up in flames just to be able to accuse her?'

His tone was vexed. 'Don't be silly! What do you expect me to say? How do you think I should react? I've known her all my life.'

Heatedly she said, 'And so that makes her a saint?'

He clenched his mouth tighter and then said in a more conciliatory tone, 'Of course not. I'm sure you didn't make this up, and I don't think that you're vindictive either. What happened is appalling, and I wish it hadn't. I just hope your idea that Mariella was the culprit is wrong.'

'Someone was riding nearby when it happened. You and Mariella are the only people I've seen on horses around the estate! I don't think it was you. You need me to finish the paintings.'

His colour increased and the skin over his cheeks tightened. 'You're getting hysterical. I'm trying to tell you that you can't make accusations without proof.'

There was a moment's silence before she glared at him. 'How dare you suggest that I'm hysterical? I am not. I haven't told this to anyone else. I wouldn't have told you either, but you insisted on finding out what I was thinking. I wish I'd kept my mouth shut now.'

He stared at Emma in silence for a moment, his mouth a thin line of annoyance.

She held his gaze. Her eyes flared and her voice was sharper. 'Your attitude only makes me furious. Why are you so gu — ' Emma intended to say 'gullible' and realized she was in danger of saying something unforgivable. She turned away for a moment and tried to calm down. 'You trust her too much. I see her with different eyes. I only told you what I heard and saw. If I'd wanted to cause trouble I wouldn't have stopped your mother calling the police.' She met his glance. 'There's no point in any further discussion. I have no real proof and I won't mention it to anyone else. You believe she isn't capable of doing something like that? Okay! I'll avoid her from now on. But when you next see her, please tell her I won't be going on any more lonely excursions again until I've finished my work.' On the brink of tears, she mused that he hadn't even asked about the burns. He'd questioned her honesty. Why had she fallen in love with someone who was so blind to reality? 'Perhaps you'll be good enough to close the door on the way out.'

His dark eyes flashed and his expression was full of fury. His hands formed to tight fists. He moved towards the door and then stopped in mid-stride to inhale an audible deep breath before he turned back to her again. The very air seemed electrified as he drew nearer, making her senses spin. He pulled her into his arms and his mouth covered hers hungrily. Giving herself to the pleasure and passion, she almost forgot about Mariella. She tried to resist him but he roused her passion, and shivers of desire raced through her instead.

'Leandro!' Franca's voice was somewhere nearby and she was coming closer. 'Leandro!'

Opening her eyes, Emma returned to reality. She gazed into his face and with longing at his sensual lips. The smouldering passion in his dark eyes made her insides jangle. He caught hold of her upper arms and pushed her gently away from him.

'Damn it! What does she want? Now of all times.'

Emma licked her lips and watched as he stepped back and ran his hand down his face.

'I'd better go; she won't give up until she finds me.' She nodded silently. With a parting look, he said, 'This talk is not over, Emma. I want you to understand exactly why I'm sceptical and why I think we need proof if it was Mariella.' He turned and hurried outside.

She heard Franca talking to him

excitedly and then going off in the direction of the house again. She leaned against the table to regain her composure and her pride.

20

A minute or so later Emma walked out of the shed and went to the garden, after checking no one else was in sight.

The garden was her haven. She walked the pathways until she finally sat down in her secluded corner. What should she do? He must realize by now that she was his for the taking. However tempted she was to accept whatever he offered of himself, she wouldn't let their relationship slide into a clandestine, hole-in-the-corner love affair. She had no intention of sharing him, however much she loved him. Clearly Mariella could do no wrong in his eyes, and Mariella would be here when Emma returned to her previous life in London. The knowledge left her with an immense feeling of despair.

There was only one answer: she had to hasten developments. She would leave as soon as possible to avoid a situation that was getting too complicated and humiliating. The work on the second painting was almost finished. Maurice would jump at the chance to take over. His leg was better.

Seeing how much he wanted to protect Mariella, Leandro might even be glad when she left. It would solve the problem of the increasing personal tension between them. She'd pointed her finger at his girlfriend and he wouldn't forget that. What she felt emotionally about him, or what she'd told him about what Mariella had done, wasn't relevant in his future plans.

She could leave the tools and equipment where they were and fly home from Pisa. Maurice could replace her and bring the jeep and everything back when he was finished.

Feeling relieved, she hurried back to the workshop and her computer. She set things in motion and contacted Maurice. It was easier to formulate an email than to talk to him personally.

She suggested the warm weather would do him good and the sun would help the healing process. She explained that she missed her flat and her friends and hoped he'd take over the third restoration job.

It didn't take long for Maurice to reply. He sounded surprised, but pleased. There was plenty of work waiting for her in the company and if she wanted to come back to London, it was okay with him. Once she'd booked her flight, he'd book his. Emma immediately booked her ticket via the internet. She fixed a flight leaving in three days' time.

The evening meal was a silent one. Marco was still out with his girlfriend and Leandro was missing too.

Zarah asked, 'How are the burns?'

'Much better. They don't hurt anymore. Your ointment did wonders.'

Zarah nodded. 'An old recipe that's been passed down through the centuries. I always have some ready, just in case. Franca told me how shocked Enzo was when he found you.'

Emma smiled. 'I can imagine. I looked a sight. I was so relieved when he found me.'

'I still wonder if it wouldn't have been better to call the police. Nothing like that has ever happened here before. It could be someone who'll perhaps try it again.'

Arranging her knife and fork tidily, Emma reassured her, 'Perhaps it was meant to be a practical joke and who-ever it was didn't realize how dangerous it was. I think I'll have an early night. If you'll excuse me, I'll skip the rest of the meal.'

Zarah nodded. 'I've had enough too. There's a good film on TV this evening. Marco is out with his girlfriend, and Leandro is helping a good friend who's in trouble.' Emma's questioning look encouraged her to add, 'A large wine vat has developed a crack and they are trying to solve the problem. Either the wine will have to be pumped into a spare vat — and you can imagine how difficult it would be to find one of a suitable size — or they'll have to find a way of sealing the crack temporarily without it damaging the quality of the wine.'

Emma nodded and got up. 'Good night.'

Zarah eyed her carefully. 'Sleep well, Emma. Remember, you are safe now.'

* * *

Next morning Emma started work early and carried on steadily until she stopped for breakfast. She heard that Leandro was still helping his friend and hadn't been back all night. She carried on as long as possible until she thought the heat might damage the process. She was clearing her things to one side in the shed when she spotted Leandro's jeep coming up the driveway. She didn't see him later when she went back to the house.

* * *

She heard that they'd saved the wine with a temporary repair and Leandro was catching up on his sleep. She was almost relieved that she didn't see him. Emma had decided she would tell them tomorrow evening that she was leaving.

* * *

She was surprised to notice Leandro's car already speeding down the road towards the highway when she was on her way to her workshop next morning. Later on when she visited the kitchen, Franca told her he had a pre-arranged meeting with a wholesaler today and he was late leaving for the appointment. The company headquarters were close to Rome and he would stay overnight with Rosella before coming back late tomorrow. Emma stared unseeingly at her coffee and realized she'd never see him again.

That evening when she told Zarah and Marco she was leaving, Leandro's mother was lost for words. 'Why? Does

Leandro know you're leaving?'

'No, I didn't have the chance to tell him. Maurice is fit enough now to replace me, and Leandro knows that Maurice intended to take over if he could. I'll miss you all and I've loved being here, but my boss will finish the last painting, as arranged.'

'Leandro is going to be very annoyed. There's nothing wrong between you and Leandro, is there? Has he upset you? Did he say something wrong?'

Emma tried to sound cheery. 'No. I haven't talked much to him much since the fire at the cottage, but there's nothing wrong.'

His mother paused. 'This has something to do with that fire, doesn't it? You're still frightened.'

Impulsively, Emma covered the older woman's hands with her own. 'I'll only remember the good things. The fire has nothing to do with it. I'll never forget Tuscany — the wonderful scenery, Franca's cooking, or your hospitality. You've treated me like a welcome guest.

I'm putting the second painting back into its frame this morning and I'll hang it before I leave. Maurice will be in touch to let you know exactly when he intends to arrive.'

Zarah's eyes were worried and her forehead wrinkled. Marco just sat and watched her carefully.

★　★　★

Franca hugged Emma when she heard. Next morning, Emma gave in when Zarah insisted that if she was leaving and needed to get to the airport, the least they could do was to make sure she got there on time. In the end, her hand luggage had included bottles of tomato jam, Villa Bella Rosa Chianti, and olive oil. She expected the airport security staff would confiscate the lot when she checked in, but she didn't want to hurt Franca's or Zarah's feelings.

Looking back up the dusty road, she waved to the two women standing together next to the villa, when Marco began the journey to Pisa Airport. There were tears at the back of her eyes and she steeled herself not to cry.

Marco looked across briefly. 'Okay?' She nodded.

He was silent for a moment and then he looked across again and said, 'I never thought my brother was stupid, but now I'm beginning to wonder.'

'What do you mean?'

'You don't have to pretend with me, *bella*. I'm an expert in sensing when the electricity flows between two people. I thought you two were heading in the right direction. I don't know what happened, but he's botched it, hasn't he? He manages the estate like a well-oiled machine, but he can't handle women. He's going to be mad when he finds out you've left, but it serves him right.'

She didn't comment and stared ahead. Marco concentrated on the road. The radio was playing softly and Emma tried to memorize the appearance of the fields and places they passed in the early-morning sunshine.

He asked suddenly, 'You do like him, don't you?'

She swallowed a lump in her throat. 'Yes, of course I like him. I like you. I like your whole family.'

'But you like some of us more than others, don't you, *bella*?' He reached across and ruffled her hair.

Without replying, she said, 'Don't wait when we get to the airport. It's probably difficult to find somewhere to park. I'll be fine. I'm used to managing on my own.'

The traffic increased noticeably the closer they came to the airport. Approaching the departure area, they saw a long, untidy column of people carrying placards, waving banners, and shouting slogans.

Marco looked for a moment and then across at Emma with a twinkle in his eye. 'It looks like this is as far as I can go. Can I leave you here?'

'Of course. I only need to get my things from the boot. Don't get out. I'll manage. Drive straight on.' She looked around. 'I wonder what the fuss is about. Thanks for everything, Marco. Take care of yourself.' She gave him a peck on his cheek and got out.

21

Pulling her suitcase, she struggled through the crowd to an entrance. She expected it to be quieter inside, but it wasn't. Instead she faced a mass of people bustling about, and lots of noise. Passengers were shouting at fellow travellers and pulling their luggage in all directions.

Emma stopped in surprise but forced on as others tried to pass her, coming in or going out. Above the sound of excited and agitated voices, she listened to a repetitive loudspeaker announcement in Italian, English and French that the airport's ground personnel were on a twenty-four-hour strike.

She should have checked before they set out. No one at the Villa Bella Rosa had known, otherwise Franca or Zarah would have told her to wait. There was no point in worrying now. If the strike was already in progress, it was merely a question of time until normal services were restored. She had to confirm her position and then find somewhere to wait. She could only hope it didn't take too long before she was airborne. Leaving Italy and Leandro was painful enough without having to prolong the agony.

After joining a long queue of others at the information desk, a harassed employee told her that the loudspeaker system would inform everyone as soon as services returned to normal. The strike had started at 6 a.m. that day. Emma wandered around, pulling her suitcase and looking for somewhere to stop. It might take hours or a whole day, so she needed somewhere quiet if that was possible. There was no point in looking for a vacant seat; each and every one was fully occupied. Emma kept walking and dodging other people until she reached the far end of the building. It was a bit quieter there, although she could still hear the announcements. She settled down in a corner. Dumping her suitcase, she was grateful that she'd be able to rest her back against a wall. Ruffling through her hand luggage, she found a thin cardigan to sit on. The people nearby all exchanged sympathetic looks among themselves. A kind of fellowship ensued. They kept an eye on each other's property if someone went to the toilet or in search of something to eat or drink.

Emma tried to avoid thinking about Leandro, but after a while that became impossible. She had too much time and nothing else to do. The fact that she would never see him again increased her misery enormously. She remembered the weeks she'd spent at his home and how her love had grown despite all her efforts to sidestep it. She thought about Mariella's ultimately successful attempts to sabotage their friendship.

It didn't help when she imagined that he might end up married to his childhood friend after all. Mariella wasn't right for him; he deserved someone better, but he wasn't stupid and it was his choice. She stared ahead and wrapped her arms around herself. She tried vainly to concentrate on other things.

Her misery was intense and her anguish succeeded in giving her a pounding headache. She'd never coped with anything similar before; but then, she'd never loved someone like this before either. She'd loved him and left him without saying goodbye. His face haunted her memory. She thought about his smile, his thoughtfulness and his teasing looks. She'd never be able to forget him. Life without Leandro had no meaning.

Minutes and hours passed and like all the other people around her, she had to get up and walk around sometimes to stretch her cramped legs and aching muscles. The strikers were still marching up and down outside; she watched them through the window. They were endearingly Italian. The bright sunshine covered them, and everything around them. It must be very tiring, walking back and forth in the heat like that. The sun made her think how her own future would be: dismal and bleak.

She turned away and began to wind her way back to her luggage. She'd gone a few steps when she bumped into someone and looked up to apologise. It was Leandro, and she stopped breathing for a moment.

She fought to control her emotions as she looked at those familiar dark eyes. Where was the solid, self-controlled and independent woman she used to be? He didn't need to even touch her to confuse her thoughts and set her whole body on fire.

'You?' she asked rather stupidly.

In the middle of her shocked silence, he said, 'Yes, me! Hello, Emma.'

She hesitated and he put an arm around her shoulder and pulled her to a nearby corner where they were comparatively alone. She looked at him, still feeling the shock. He grabbed her hands and his nearness robbed her of sensible thoughts.

Her pulse rate was increasing by the second and she prayed he didn't notice the effect he was having. She reminded herself that this man believed in another woman more than he did in her. Her face was white and she felt stunned. She managed to ask, 'What are you doing here?'

He bent his head and his breath fanned her face before his lips touched hers like a whisper, and shattered her resistance. His eyelashes touched her cheek briefly, then she stared up at him and willed herself to remain unresponsive. She managed to keep her emotions under a semblance of control until his mouth swooped to capture hers again, but then her mouth moved hungrily under his.

He murmured, 'That was all I wanted to know. You ran away from me, and I understand why, but don't pretend you don't like me. Your kiss tells me something else!' His arms encircled her waist and he whispered into her hair. 'Why didn't you wait until we could talk about everything?'

She looked at him and still couldn't believe he was here. She licked her lips. 'We tried that, didn't we? I thought it was better to get out of the way. For my sake as well as yours. I've arranged for Maurice to come and finish the commission.'

He nodded absent-mindedly before he ran his hands up her body and held her tightly. 'I know. My mother told me what you said and what you did. I only wish you'd waited.' His dark eyes and serious expression were full of deliberation. '*Cara mia*, I first have to explain why I held back in telling you how much you mean to me. I decided to wait for you to officially finish the work before I did. I must admit the attraction was so strong that I gave in to temptation now and then. I never thought I'd ever fall in love so fast and forever, but I have. I don't know exactly how or when it happened, but it did. I waited impatiently because I didn't want you to think I was another employer taking advantage. I wanted you to understand what I felt for you had nothing to do with business. I wanted you to be as free as I was, to make up your own mind about whether we belonged together, or not.'

Emma wanted to grab something to steady herself, but she couldn't because his face and his body were too close. She was tightly imprisoned within his arms and was honest enough to realize she didn't want to resist. Her body told her this was what she longed for. It was incredible, unbelievable, and so unexpected. He bent his head to kiss her again and this time it was a challenge and she responded. The pit of her stomach whirled and she closed her eyes to enjoy the feeling of his lips on hers. Raising his head, he looked into her eyes and was almost triumphant before his next kiss feathered the surface of her lips like a summer breeze. It left her burning with desire and weak at the knees. Laughing softly he kissed the tip of her nose, then her eyes and then her mouth again.

Her eyes flashed. 'Leandro, please! This is madness!'

He straightened and his eyes were full of mischief. 'Does your 'please' mean you want more, or that you want me to stop? If it is madness, then I'll be content to be a madman for the rest of my life.' He drew her even closer to him until she felt they were one.

Emma swallowed hard and tried to manage a suitable answer. It took too long.

With a fiery expression, he said, 'You were perfectly right to feel disappointed about my reactions the last time we talked about the fire at the cottage. I was confused, shocked and scared about what you'd gone through. I realize now it probably all sounded like I was sympathizing with Mariella and didn't care about you, or that I didn't believe what you told me. Please, forgive me for that, and try to understand why. I've known Mariella all my life. I couldn't believe she was responsible for anything so horrific.

'I was on the brink of telling you that I intended to dig for the truth until I found it, when Franca came searching for me because a friend of mine needed help. I went, thinking I still had plenty of time to sort it out later. You'd already said you wouldn't take any more risks, so I thought you'd be safe until I could find out who did it.' Emma squirmed in his arms, but he held her tight. 'I like Mariella's father and her brother. They are hard-working, respectable men. I knew they wouldn't settle for less than absolute proof that Mariella had acted like a madwoman. I had to be sure before I confronted them.'

She said determinedly, 'So you were worried about Mariella's family? That's very praiseworthy. What about me? Why do you think I would accuse Mariella of something so dreadful, unless I thought it might be true? I tried to tell you that but you just brushed it aside, didn't you?'

He studied her thoughtfully for a while and stroked some strands of hair off her face. 'Yes, I did think your emotions were a bit out of control at that moment because of what had happened. It didn't mean I brushed your words aside. I'm not stupid, Emma. When Franca told me Mariella had warned you to stay away from me I realized Mariella was jealous and had an absurd illusion that I'd ask her to marry me one day. In her own way, I think she even believes she loves me — that is, as far as she can love anyone. Perhaps she's been expecting it for too long already and your arrival, and my interest in you, drove her over the edge.

'I remembered how Mariella started making critical remarks about you at about the same time as she warned you off. I told her to stop it because they weren't justified. I was in love with you by then. She stopped doing that, but it must have indicated where things were heading. She probably started thinking about some other way to get rid of you.'

His hands explored the soft lines of her back, her waist and her hips. 'After I heard about the fire at the cottage and you told me about your suspicions, I was angry, furious and felt helpless because I hadn't registered the danger signs and hadn't protected you.

'You believed I was on her side, but I wasn't. Before I left for that meeting with our wholesalers in Rome, I went over to the Lorenzos'. She wasn't at home but it was easy to find the evidence. She'd stacked it away in a corner of the stable — a canister of petrol and some scraps of material. When I compared them to the bits of rags from the bottle thrown into the cottage, there was no doubt that they were the same. I told her father what I'd found. We had an uncomfortable talk. He agreed to let me check the computer. The copy of the email she sent you was still stored there. She didn't even go to the trouble of deleting it. She'd created a new email address using Alessa's name.

'The two of us confronted her, and I threatened to go to the police. Her father begged me to let him send her away to live with some distant relatives. I agreed but I made her sign an admission, in case she ever thinks about coming back or taking revenge. She realizes she'll face a very long jail sentence if she ever does, so you don't need to be afraid. She's already left, and now I want you to come back with me.'

Her own desire growing, Emma tried in vain to free herself from his embrace and think logically. Her pulse was out of control. She tried to remain annoyed with him, but a thrill of anticipation touched her heart. Floundering, she spluttered, 'Come back? Why do you think I'd want to come back?'

'Because I hope there'll be a happy end for us both. You are the only woman I've ever wanted to marry. I'm hoping that you'll be generous and agree to live with me here in Italy. I can't leave the estate at present because there's still a real danger that my mother, and the others, will end up destitute. Marco isn't yet capable of running the estate on his own; you know that. I want you; I want you to come back and live with me. If you don't, my whole life will be pointless. If you want to go on with your work, I'll find the money for air-conditioning and for dust-free cabinets. There must be thousands of pictures in Tuscany waiting to be restored. I'll do anything to keep you here.

'I'm begging you to forgive me if you thought I didn't trust you or believe you! I was a damned fool not to explain properly that I was suspicious too, and that I intended to get the bottom of it all. I'll do everything to make you happy if you give me the chance. I need you, Emma!'

Silently she looked at him, and then her voice wavered. 'Do you realize just how much it mattered that it looked like you didn't support me when I needed you?'

He replied in a constricted voice, 'Dear heart, what can I do to make up for my stupidity — for not explaining that I would confront Mariella and that I'd find the truth? I'll do anything.'

'Swear to me that you will never, ever doubt me again.'

'I swear! I was about to clear things with you when Franca came to tell me my friend needed help. After visiting the Lorenzos' next day to pin Mariella, I had to leave for Rome straight away. I didn't have time to tell you what I'd discovered. I thought I'd have all the time in the world when I came back. I was devastated when Marco told me he'd just taken you to the airport. He made me walk on hot coals and told me I'd never acted more stupidly, before he finally let me off the hook and said there was a strike in progress and you'd probably be stuck at the airport for the rest of the day.' His wonderful smile unfurled and then he kissed her again. 'Do I have a chance? Can we please talk about our future and about us? I wonder if I'd told Mariella outright that I was in love with you, she would have accepted it.'

'I don't think so. She wanted you for herself. She wanted to drive a wedge between us and she hoped I'd die here, or just go home again.'

His lips were a thin line. 'Don't remind me of what might have happened! I want to forget her. She was desperate and slightly crazy. I love you, and I hope that you love me. That's all that matters to me now.'

Any remaining resistance was slowly melting away. Emma wanted this man. Hesitatingly, she looked at his adored face. 'Yes, I love you. I wasn't looking for love; I didn't expect to find it in Italy, and I didn't even think I needed anyone until we met.' The colour rose in her face. She realized that this wasn't a daydream — it was happening. Leandro was here and he loved her. More confident now, she wound her arms inside his jacket and around his back.

His eyes showed approval and he cradled her more tightly in his arms. 'The estate isn't a goldmine — it never will be, but we can have a good life together.'

Emma untangled one of her hands and placed her fingers over his mouth. 'How very old-fashioned and silly you are sometimes. The estate is beautiful and you run it like clockwork. We'll have a wonderful life together.'

He stroked the hair out of her face. 'I don't want to deny you anything but I'm asking you to give up your homeland, your family, and your friends and come to live with me in the Villa Bella Rosa.'

She reached up on tiptoe and kissed him. 'A flight from Pisa to London takes two hours. I don't live with my parents anymore and haven't for years; I'll probably see more of them if I come to you than I did before. They'll be sun-hungry visitors. And once I've learned some Italian, I hope I'll make new friends.'

He lifted her from the floor and swung her around a little. 'Oh, Emma! Life is going to be wonderful.' Setting her down again and running his finger down her cheek, he added, 'Do you realize that my mother, Franca and Marco are expecting me to bring you back? Marco told me I was stupid not to tell you how I felt a short time ago, and he was right of course. I think Mama and Franca both decided that you were perfect for me ages ago.'

Her eyes widened. 'Really?'

'Oh, remember to cancel Maurice's visit. If he makes a fuss, I'll find him a holiday home for a couple of weeks. The Villa Bella Rosa is waiting for you, not for him.' His voice was velvet and his expression seductive. 'We may have to resort to a little subterfuge now and then until we get married, because otherwise Franca will start lecturing us, but I'm sure we'll find a way around that problem.' His grin was infectious and she felt the magnetism that had drawn them together from the start.

Her feelings for him had nothing to do with logic or reason, but she did try to be sensible. Emma tilted her head. 'Are you sure you love me?'

He crushed her to him. 'I'm more certain about that than anything else in my life. If you'll have me, I want to spend the rest of my life with you.'

She nodded and said softly, 'I didn't realize something was lacking until I met you. I'm so grateful that fate brought us together.'

Her body ached for his touch. She snuggled closer.

He pleaded, 'Can we get out of this place and go home now?'

THE END